KT-234-964

2200003874
NEATH PORT TALBOT

A Safe Place
to Kill

A Safe Place
to Kill

Nicholas J. Clough

ROBERT HALE · LONDON

© Nicholas J. Clough 2008
First published in Great Britain 2008

ISBN 978-0-7090-8557-7

Robert Hale Limited
Clerkenwell House
Clerkenwell Green
London EC1R 0HT

www.halebooks.com

The right of Nicholas J. Clough to be identified as
author of this work has been asserted by him
in accordance with the Copyright, Designs and
Patents Act 1988

2 4 6 8 10 9 7 5 3 1

NEATH PORT TALBOT LIBRARIES	
2200003874	
Bertrams	30/10/2008
M	£18.99
RES	

Typeset in 11½/16pt Palatino
by Derek Doyle & Associates, Shaw Heath
Printed and bound in Great Britain
by Biddles Limited, King's Lynn

CHAPTER ONE

L ATE at night. when there was a strange, hollow knocking in the vestry and the wind moaned through the graveyard, nobody went near the church.

In daylight it was an unremarkable building. A low greystone building with a tiled pitched roof and, at the base of the clock tower, a heavy oak door hung on large hinges, the hinge straps once black, now the colour of rusty age and neglect. The clarion of bells in the tower had long since gone, but the clock still worked. Once the only timepiece in the village, now it kept very bad time and hardly anybody even glanced at it. Locals talked about the dark legend that there was something evil in the church. Events were about to prove them right.

In the graveyard at the back of the church Trevor Wilkins spat on his hands, picked up a spade and began to dig. He had been the sexton for nearly ten years and he liked to do things the old fashioned way.

He sank the blade into a rectangle of earth he had measured out by slicing off a thin layer of turf. He dug with an obsessive mechanical routine, his eyes never moving from the ground in front of him, the spadesful of dirt thrown in piston precision on to a neat, growing mound to one side of the grave. He was knee deep in earth before he paused and wiped his brow. There was not as much sweat as last week, the days must be getting cooler. He took a soiled red hand-kerchief from his pocket and ran it across the back of his neck. Then he looked up at the sky. A strengthening westerly wind, blowing the first dried leaves in patterns between the grave-stones, like children playing tag, was bringing clouds in a darkening sky.

There was a fresh chill in the air. Autumn had crept up behind summer and barged it out of the way. The long summer evenings of picnics on Saxons Mound, swapping gossip round the wooden tables in front of The Feathers and barbeques on the back lawn, were over for another year. The harvest was in, the season had turned and the land was beginning to settle down for the winter.

He turned back to his digging. In two hours the ground would be ready to receive the wooden coffin, the priest would say a blessing, the relatives pay their respects and when they had all gone, unnoticed he would return to pile the soil back into the grave. He paused again, his head raising and turning, his eyes darting like a hunted animal. What was that noise? It seemed to come from the church. Was it the wind? He went back to his work and gave an involuntary shudder. Perhaps that was the wind as well. He hoped so.

Ten miles away in the small town of Shapford, Thomas Charles Daykin, Inspector of Police, read and signed the last report on his desk and tossed it into the out tray. There was a single sheet of white paper left on the desk. Daykin picked it up and, leaning back and putting his feet on the desk, he care-fully folded into a dart. He held it up to eye level and looked along its length. Then he turned the nose up at an angle and launched the dart across the room. It flew in a graceful upward curve before stalling and diving nose down, landing on the neck of a large Old English Sheepdog that had been lying silently, its head on its paws, for the last two hours.

The dog looked up expectantly through the white mophead of hair that fell from the top of its head.

'Just a short walk, Royston,' said Daykin.

He was getting up from his seat and the dog was already sitting facing the door when the phone rang. Daykin leant forward and picked it up.

'Daykin, a word. In my office. Now, please.'

The phone went dead. Superintendent Jarvis, a man so self-important that nobody knew his first name.

'Sorry, Royston.' he said to the dog, 'The walk will have to wait.'

It gave him its most reproving look and padded back to the corner where it laid down with its back to him.

'Later, I promise.'

The dog ignored him.

Superintendent Jarvis had spent years cultivating the look of a country squire. He dressed in three-piece tweed suits highly polished brown brogues and ties that looked vaguely regimental. His office was full of prints of fox hunting, fishing and horse racing. On the mantelpiece stood five silver cups. If anyone had looked carefully they would have found that everything was fake. The suits and shoes looked handmade, but were off the peg. The ties had been designed and made in a workshop in Malaysia. Only his wife knew that he had never been anywhere near a horse or a fishing rod and the cups had been bought as a job lot in Portobello Road.

At his office door Tom Daykin did what Jarvis had ruled to be required practice. He knocked at the door and waited.

'Come,' said Jarvis's voice from inside.

Daykin opened the door and walked in. His professional life had flashed before him all the way down the corridor. No one was blameless, but he couldn't work out what Jarvis wanted with him. All he knew was that when Jarvis issued one of his summonses it was never good news.

'Ah, Daykin, said Jarvis as if he hadn't expected him. 'Come and sit you down.' He liked expressions like 'Come and sit you down' and he let the words roll round his mouth before he said them.

There was one wooden chair placed directly in front of the desk and Daykin sat upright on it while Jarvis stared silently at him across the desk, gently rocking in the comfort of his executive leather armchair.

'I have a job for you.'

'I have a lot on at the moment, sir,' said Daykin. He was just making conversation, nothing he had ever said had made Superintendent Jarvis change his mind.

'This isn't a crime to solve, this is' – Jarvis savoured the words – 'a bit of babysitting.'

'A bit of what?'

Jarvis ignored the question and opened a buff file on his desk.

'Headquarters are transferring to us a young detective sergeant for a six-month secondment. He's been fast tracked,' continued Jarvis, scanning the file. 'University degree, joined the force as a graduate eighteen months ago.'

'Eighteen months to detective sergeant,' said Daykin, 'that's fast, even for a graduate.'

Jarvis looked up from the file.

'His father is the assistant chief constable.

'So,' continued Jarvis, 'we all have to be on our best behaviour; we don't want any tales being told over the family dining-table, do we?'

'When does he get here?'

'This afternoon.'

'What's his name?'

'Toby Peterson.'

Jarvis closed the file and looked at Daykin.

'That's all,' he said, in case Daykin was thinking about staying. 'When he arrives I'll do the usual introductions, settle him in and then bring him down to your office.'

Daykin got up to leave.

'Daykin,' said Jarvis, screwing his eyes up questioningly, 'you haven't brought that dog of yours in again, have you?'

'He gets lonely on his own.'

'Well, get rid of him by lunchtime, this is a police station, not an animal sanctuary.'

On his way back to the office Daykin found his way blocked by Chief Inspector Sykes. She was tall – perhaps 5'9" – and slim but when she stood in the middle of the corridor there was no getting round her. She looked at him with cool detachment. Daykin stared back, not sure what to say.

Paula Sykes had transferred to North Yorkshire from the West Midlands force about six months ago, saying that she wanted to get away from the city. She spent most of her spare time walking the Dales with all the enthusiasm of a recent convert. Her uniform was impeccable: knife sharp creases down the trousers and jacket sleeves, buttons, whistle chain and shoes shining and not a spot or stain on anything. Her chestnut hair, which might be naturally curly and artificially straightened, was pulled back into a tight bun on the back of her head.

Only one thing spoilt her wide eyed, high-cheekboned face.

A small white scar, which she didn't attempt to hide with make-up, ran from the left corner of her mouth to the jawline. When she smiled the right side of her mouth curved upwards and a dimple appeared in her cheek, but the left side remained in a stubborn straight line.

Daykin hadn't seen much of her, she spent most of her time alone in her office she was a deskbound administrator. She didn't use the canteen or go down to the local pub after her shift. There were rumours of a love affair that had gone badly wrong, but that was only because nobody knew anything about her, so they started rumours.

'Everything all right?' she asked.

'I've just been told that I'm babysitting the assistant chief constable's son for a while.'

'I heard he was coming. Bad luck. The best you can hope for is that you do absolutely everything right. If you need any help, let me know.'

She was gone before Daykin could thank her. Everything about her made people think she would march off, arms swinging like a soldier at a passing-out parade, but she glided with a natural swing of her hips that catwalk models have to be taught.

Daykin walked back to his office. As he opened the door the dog looked up expectantly.

'Let's go for that walk,' said Daykin. 'But enjoy it, I've a feeling you are going to spend the afternoon in the back of the car.'

CHAPTER TWO

Back in Camleigh, Revd Robert Morton stopped his old compact car by the kerb and switched off the engine. He looked through the car window at the church. He was the rural dean. in charge of four country parishes and St Peters was the smallest and most neglected of them all. The congregations were always tiny, often uninterested and, in the dark hours of the soul he had to admit, he resented coming here. Today was routine, just checking the church on his way past. He would be in and out in fifteen minutes and could be home early for tea. Perhaps an extra glass of sherry tonight.

He got out of the car and paused under the roof of the lych gate to check that his keys were in his pocket. Then he walked along the narrow cobbled path to the oak door. He put the key he had selected into the lock and turned it. There was no resistance and not the usual dull click as the lock disengaged. Then he saw the damage to the door. In fear and frustration he turned the handle and the door swung open slowly. He stepped into the church and stopped by the font to listen. The church was silent. He walked quickly to the vestry and checked the small safe. Unlike the door, it was locked. He opened it. Inside, in a green canvas bag, was the collection

11

from last Sunday. He felt the weight of it in his hand. Hardly worth taking anyway. He checked the case which should contain six bottles of communion wine. All correct. Then it hit him. The silver gilt altar candlesticks and the seventeenth-century painting of the Madonna and Child, all on or near the altar, would be the first things a thief would take. He strode out of the vestry and up the aisle towards the altar.

The candlesticks and painting were exactly where they had been for years. It wasn't that there was something missing, something was there that shouldn't be. Lying with his head facing the altar and his feet to the nave, his eyes staring blankly up at the fan ceiling of the church was his senior churchwarden Michael Hilliam. And then he saw the blood. It came from his mouth and nose and from a gaping wound in his left side that stained the once blue shirt to a deep purple. It oozed from under the body and had spread across the carpet in a miniature dark brown lake. Robert Morton put one hand to his mouth in horror and shock. He tried to sink to one knee in prayer, something he should do by instinct and training, but instead he leant quickly forward and vomited violently over the side of the front pew.

'Come and sit you down, Toby,' said Jarvis, pointing to a chair with padded seat and arms that had replaced the chair of the Inquisition that Daykin had sat on earlier.

'Tea?' asked Jarvis, holding up a silver teapot. He kept a china tea service in the small cupboard in the corner of the room in case important guests arrived.

Jarvis spent twenty minutes asking polite but probing questions about the young man's father, questions which were just as politely deflected, then they went on a short tour round the station, ending at the door of Daykin's office.

'This is the office of the inspector who'll look after you from now. He's a bit of a rough diamond, but he knows the area and he's a good thief taker. He'll show you a lot about police work.'

He knocked on the door, which he didn't normally do, and opened it.

Daykin was sitting at his desk, pretending to look through a file he had read five times, when he heard the knock at the door and Superintendent Jarvis walked in, followed by a young man six inches taller and twenty-five years younger.

'This is Toby Peterson.' said Jarvis, stepping aside and in the silence before anyone said anything gave Daykin the chance to take a look at the time bomb that had been put in his lap. He was about twenty-five years old, tall and casually but expensively dressed. Clear blue eyes and a strong jaw. He stood upright with a straight back that, with the blond hair cut very short, gave him the look of a soldier. He was young but had the air of a golden child, confident and assured. Daykin decided to dislike him.

'I'm Tom Daykin,' he said, getting up to offer his hand.

'Toby Peterson, but you know that,' replied the young man, shaking his hand. The handshake was firm, the voice was mellow and he smiled when he spoke. Despite himself, Daykin had to admit it was a good start.

They talked about the town and the station for ten minutes before Jarvis looked at his watch.

'I've got a meeting in five minutes,' he said, getting up suddenly. 'I'll leave you now. Show him the ropes, Tom.'

Now Daykin was sure that he had been stitched like a kipper. Jarvis never called him 'Tom'.

*

Daykin had never been the centre of cocktail parties and his small talk was very small. As he struggled to keep the conversation with Toby Peterson alive, Robert Morton was half running, half staggering along the path from the church, holding a bright yellow handkerchief to his mouth and pausing every ten yards to retch into it. How far he would have got he would never know because, doubled up in pain and despair, he heard the lych gate handle turn and saw, out of the corner of one watering eye, Siobahn Murgatroyd walking towards him, her arms full of the cut flowers she was going to arrange in the church.

If he had hand picked someone to look after a crisis, it would have been Miss Murgatroyd. In her late sixties and retired from a lifelong career as an officer in the Women's Military Nursing Corps, she had the skills of a nurse and the hardened attitudes of an army officer.

'Vicar,' she said, dropping the flowers in a heap on the path and placing two practiced hands on his shoulders, 'Straighten up and take deep breaths.'

Even if he had not felt so weak he would not have been able to resist her firm push. While he sucked air slowly into his lungs, she took a long, hard look at him.

'What on earth has caused this?' she said, her voice as firm as her grip.

He pointed to the church, still not able to speak. With a gentleness that owed more to training than choice, she guided him to a wooden bench and sat him down.

'You wait there,' she said, and walked towards the church door which still stood open, where he had thrown it back in his haste to escape. Chivalry was part of his make-up and he knew that he should not let her go into the church alone, but he was still feeling weak and nauseous and he knew that she wasn't going to wait to let him recover.

Siobahn Murgatroyd stepped over the threshold of the church.

'Is anyone there?' she shouted.

There was a noise from the clock tower which stopped her in her tracks. She waited, straining every nerve, but the sound did not repeat itself, so she took a tentative step forward. There was a pair of scissors in a pot on a table just to the right of the door. They were for the flower arrangers. She would have used them later to cut the flowers she had brought with her, but now she picked them up and held them in front of her like a dagger.

Armed, and possibly dangerous, she walked slowly into the body of the church, all her senses on high alert, the adrenalin coursing through her veins. Then she saw what Revd Morton had seen. She recognized the body immediately and, still watchful, she strode up the aisle towards it.

She had been in the presence of death and those on the point of death many times and it had long ago ceased to distress her. Where Revd Morton had failed in the presence of the body to fall back on his training, she succeeded. She knelt down and, although she already knew the answer, she reached out with her left hand and felt the right side of his neck. There was no pulse and she could feel the first sign of rigor mortis settling into the muscles.

She stood up and looked at the body with a calm professionalism. He lay on his back, his arms stretched out each side, his legs straight and placed together. He looked as if he had been crucified. The sightless eyes stared directly up at the ceiling and she noticed what Robert Morton had seen, the signs of a wound in his left side. And there was something else. His shoes and socks had been removed and there were holes in both hands and feet, like the marks of nails. Stigmata.

Her eyes not moving from the body, she reached into her jacket pocket and pulled out a mobile phone. She dialled the emergency number. While she was waiting for it to connect, she noticed something else, it was the look on his face. A mixture of pain and surprise.

'Police,' she said as the call was answered.

'Police, can I help you?'

'I want to report a murder.'

CHAPTER THREE

THE small talk, which had never got off the ground, had buried itself in a long embarrassing silence when the phone on Daykin's desk rang.

'Cut the social conversation, Inspector. I've got a job for you.' said Jarvis, 'you'd better come to my office.'

'Sit down.' said Jarvis, not looking up from the papers on the desk in front of him as they walked into his office, 'and take notes.'

Eventually he looked up from his desk and began a monologue. By the time he had finished, without a pause or his gaze leaving their faces, Daykin guessed that he had memorized the papers on his desk, word for word. It was an impressive piece of recall.

'Exactly thirty-two minutes ago,' began Jarvis, 'a Miss Siobahn Murgatroyd viewed the body of the senior churchwarden, Michael Hilliam, in St Peters church in Camleigh. He was lying on his back in the aisle, his head towards the altar. He had been dead for perhaps two hours or so. That is what Miss Murgatroyd estimates and she is a retired nurse.

'Mr Hilliam's shoes and socks had been removed and arranged by the side of the body. He'd had been stabbed in the heart and in both hands and feet. Twelve minutes before Miss Murgatroyd saw him, the body of Mr Hilliam had been discovered by Reverend Robert Morton, who had then run back up the church path where he was found in a state of some distress by Miss Murgatroyd.

'I have despatched uniformed officers to seal the church and asked for a Scenes of Crimes team and a pathologist to attend the site. Now you know as much as I do, so why don't you both scoot across there and start asking questions?'

Daykin, who had never scooted anywhere in his life, folded his notebook and put it in his jacket pocket.

'Any suspects, sir?'

'Don't be ridiculous, Inspector. The body's still warm.'

Jarvis carefully put the papers on his desk into a maroon file. Then he looked up at both of them, as if surprised to see them.

'Well,' he said, 'what are you waiting for? This case won't solve itself.'

Daykin and Peterson got up, left the office and walked out of the back door of the station to the car-park. Toby Peterson took out an electronic car key and used it to unlock a BMW in showroom condition. Daykin was tempted.

'No,' he said finally, 'I know the way, we'll go in my car.'

Toby Peterson followed Daykin to the far side of the car-park. Standing alone was an old, battered Renault saloon, rusting badly at the corners and in desperate need of a wash. Daykin put the key in the lock, got in and leaned across to open the passenger door.

'Central locking has failed,' he said, as Toby Peterson opened the door and caught an empty soft drinks can that fell from the seat.

Daykin lifted a week's supply of newspapers from the

passenger seat and threw them into the back of the car.

He got back into the driver's seat and turned the ignition key. He looked surprised when the engine fired first time.

They pulled out of the car-park and drove round the block into the high street. The humpback bridge at its far end, arching over a stretch of water too large to be a stream and too small to be a river, was the marker that they had left the town behind them. Immediately Toby Peterson saw the mosaic of green fields, criss-crossed by grey drystone walls and dotted with trees, rolling to the horizon and thought that if a man wanted to be at peace with himself and be comfortable with his existence, this wasn't the worst place in the world to live.

'What's Camleigh like?' he asked eventually.

'About twenty minutes and a thousand miles away,' said Daykin, tapping the fuel gauge and frowning at it.

'The people of Camleigh and Shapford don't get on, never have, it's something to do with village life against town life. Fortunately, nothing ever happens there, so I don't go very often, there's nothing to investigate.'

'There is now.'

'True.'

The journey to Camleigh was as slow as the pace of life. They snaked across the countryside along narrow roads barely wide enough for two vehicles to pass each other and edged on each side with banks of earth topped with the uniform grey stone walls. The journey was slowed nearly to a halt twice by flocks of sheep and once by a tractor. Toby Peterson began to shift uneasily in his seat with frustration, but Daykin took it all calmly, seeming to enjoy the distractions. Just when Peterson was on the point of swearing, they drove over the top of a hill and spread out in the valley below them was the village of Camleigh. Daykin stopped the car to give them both a chance to take a good look at the scene below them.

It was a typical Dales village. A ribbon of High Street running through a pattern of avenues of houses. Peterson could make out the pub, school and village store. And he couldn't miss the church. It stood at one end of the High Street, slightly away from the other buildings, like a socially superior guest at a wedding, on the guest list but distancing itself from the rest. Around it, swarming like ants, were ten to fifteen police officers.

Putting the car into gear, Daykin drove down the narrow, winding hill into the village. He parked behind two marked police cars. In the passenger seat of the nearest one, the door wide open and sitting sideways, facing outwards so that he could pull on a pair of wellington boots, sat a young constable. The boots were too small and he concentrated hard on pushing his feet into them. He didn't hear Daykin.

'What do you know so far, Robbo?' asked Daykin.

The young man looked up, then immediately got to his feet.

'I'm not too sure, sir. I've just got here. There's a body inside the church and I think someone's interviewing the vicar.'

'Who's in charge?' asked Daykin, looking across the churchyard to the open door of the church and the police tape that ran around the building.

'You are, sir.'

'Don't be stupid, lad. Until I arrived.' said Daykin without any malice in his voice.

'Sorry, sir. Sergeant Carter.'

'When you've got your boots on, find him and tell him I want the tapes round the whole churchyard, not just the

20

church. I don't want a busload of rubbernecks stamping all over the area.'

Daykin and Peterson walked up the cobbled pathway that Revd Morton had stumbled down less than an hour earlier. Peterson looked down at the path.

'Footprints, sir?'

Daykin kept walking and shook his head.

'Not even Sherlock Holmes with a magnifying glass could get a footprint from cobbles.'

They reached the open church door. Another young constable stood guard. He touched the peak of his cap in what passed for a salute when he saw Daykin. If Daykin was bothered about being saluted, he didn't show it.

'Who's inside, Trevor?'

Trevor looked up at the sky and creased his face into a grimace of concentration.

'Sergeant Carter, some lads from Scenes of Crimes, Dr Caisley, the vicar and Roger and Chris from Traffic.'

'What are Traffic doing here?'

'A lot of people still on holiday, sir. We're short staffed.'

Toby Peterson stood back and watched. If they had sent him out here for an education in policing country areas, he was getting it. It also gave him the chance to take a good long look at Thomas Daykin.

He must have been powerfully built in his youth and his shoulders were still broad and unbowed. But he now had the waist of a middle-aged man.

He wore a tired-looking sports jacket, not dirty, just creased and well worn. One of the buttons hung by two or three threads, in danger of dropping off with every movement Daykin made. The corduroy trousers, shiny in patches, had been bought when he was about ten pounds lighter and they struggled to keep the stomach in. Occasionally Daykin ran both thumbs round the waistband, as if that would ease the pressure of flesh against material.

Under the jacket was a grey shirt and a purple tie, the colour clashing with both jacket and shirt. Toby Peterson, who tied a half Windsor, knew a good tie knot when he saw one and Daykin's, lying at an odd angle two inches below the collar button, wasn't one of them.

Oddly, the brown shoes were both well cared for and highly polished.

'Oh, and that Murgatroyd woman is in there as well,' said the constable.

'Just when I thought I couldn't have any more fun.' said Daykin wearily, as he walked through the door. Toby Peterson followed him and they both stopped inside the doorway to let their eyes adjust to the light.

'Who is that Murgatroyd woman?' whispered Peterson.

'She's all right, but she's a retired military nursing officer, makes a civilian matron look like a doting granny.'

Before Peterson could reply, Daykin said. 'And you're about to meet her.'

Striding determinedly down the aisle and doing a smart right wheel towards them came a formidable figure in tweeds and brogues.

'Inspector, at least we'll have some sense now.' She shouted from ten yards away.

'Is there a problem, Miss Murgatroyd?' Daykin asked politely.

'Yes, there damned well is,' she said, ignoring that she was in church. 'I've been stuck here for the best part of an hour. The only person who has spoken to me is that sergeant, and all he told me to do was wait in the vestry.'

She pronounced 'sergeant' the way some military officers do, as if it is a form of pond life. 'And,' she continued, 'I have a foursome for bridge at my house tonight, so I have preparations to make.'

'This is Sergeant Peterson,' said Daykin, trying to pronounce 'sergeant' the way she had, but failing miserably. 'He will take a statement from you in the vestry and then we'll be happy to let you go home.'

Without another a word Siobahn Murgatroyd strode purposefully towards the vestry.

'From the time she saw the vicar, until the police arrived.' said Daykin to Toby Peterson. 'It shouldn't take long, she was never one to take the slow boat and today she's in one of her frantic moods. When you finish I'll be with Phil Carter.' He nodded towards the altar. 'And see if you can organize a cup of tea, will you?'

Daykin didn't go straight to the altar, he stopped at the west end of the aisle and took a long look round the church. He didn't know if he believed in God. When his wife died he had screamed at God for letting it happen, uselessly shaking his fist at Heaven and railing against the injustice of it. But why would you lose your temper with someone who doesn't exist? Anyway, he found an odd comfort in the thought of life after death. He'd been to this church perhaps half-a-dozen times over the years, weddings, baptisms and funerals, but now he took in every square inch.

The altar was draped in the green cloth of Pentecost. Behind it stood a plain marble triptych with gold leaf lattice-work and above that a stained-glass window. The glass badly needed a clean and the overcast day didn't help, but Daykin guessed that with the sun behind it, the colours would reflect bright patterns on to the aisle carpet.

Between him and the altar were rows of plain pews, the wood stained almost black with time, and running at right angles to them, two small choir stalls, each with a row of small brass lights topped with tiny red shades. The ornate pattern of beams on the ceiling contrasted with the large plain stone flags of the floor between the choir stalls.

At the back of the church were a vestry, a font, a sidesman's table and a small kitchen at the base of the clock tower. Looking into the kitchen, he heard for the first time the dull mechanical sound of the clock's pendulum as it swung with stately precision behind a pair of large oak doors. From the kitchen there was a small door that he guessed led to the back of the church and to its left, a wrought-iron spiral staircase that climbed to the organ loft immediately above him.

Daykin took one more look round him and then walked up the aisle towards a squat balding man in a badly fitting suit who was speaking quietly into a mobile telephone. He saw Daykin coming, finished the conversation and put the phone away.

'Hello, Phil, anything I need to know?'

'Not yet Tom, the doctor's been and gone and I'm waiting for the SOCO team to finish up before I move the body.'

'Any weapon found?' asked Daykin, as he knelt down to take a closer look at the body.

'I've had the lads search the church, moving outwards from the site of the body, but they found nothing, not even a spot of anyone's blood but the deceased's.'

'Someone has been very careful,' said Daykin, looking closely at the lifeless face staring up at the ceiling. 'No weapon, no witnesses, no clues. They're about to start searching the churchyard, maybe they'll come up with something.'

'I wouldn't hold my breath.'

'Did he have any family?'

'No children. A wife he divorced some years ago. I think his mother is still alive, but she's in the nursing home on Rooley Lane.'

'Send a couple of uniforms to tell mum and the wife. I don't want it coming as a surprise when they read about it in the morning papers. And tell them to ask the usual questions, enemies, debts, that sort of thing.'

Daykin looked over the body inch by inch, studying the neatly cut hair, the clean-shaven face, the white starched shirt, old school tie, sports jacket, suede waistcoat and cavalry twill trousers.

'What's this?' he said, pointing to the outstretched hands. The palm of each had been pierced. There were clean holes, from which identical rivulets of blood ran down to the floor. Daykin looked at the bare feet. Two more wounds, each filled with dried blood.

Sergeant Carter didn't reply.

Daykin got to his feet, his eyes not leaving the body.

'Stigmata,' he said.

'What?'

'The wounds of Christ. It's supposed to be a sign of deep faith.'

'I'm not a churchgoer, Tom.'

They both looked down at the body, wondering what to do next. Daykin ran his hand through his hair.

'Those aren't stigmata, Inspector,' said a voice from behind them.

Daykin turned to look at a dark silhouette, tall and pencil thin, half hidden in the deep shadow cast by one of the massive stone columns that supported the roof. The figure stepped out into the light. It was Revd Robert Morton, dressed in a simple black cassock, high at the neck and falling in straight unpleated lines to his ankles. Its blackness made his pale face seem clown white.

'Stigmata,' he said, 'are the physical manifestations of the spiritual belief, marks on the skin representing our Lord's wounds. These' – he pointed to the figure on the floor, more sorrow in his voice than horror – 'are wounds made with a weapon.'

Daykin had heard that the vicar had been distraught but now he seemed in control of himself, perhaps too much in control. Daykin took his notebook out of his pocket.

'Do you know him, Vicar?' he said, watching him as Robert Morton stared at the face looking up from the floor.

'Of course. That's Michael Hilliam, my senior churchwarden.'

CHAPTER FOUR

'Division of labour,' said Daykin as Toby Peterson came out of the vestry. 'I'll speak to the vicar and, as you've got to know Miss Murgatroyd so well over the last thirty minutes, why don't you follow her home and take some background details from her?'

Toby Peterson pulled a face. 'Why don't I see the vicar and you take the dragon lady?'

'Because you need the experience. I decide who sees who; privilege of rank.'

'But I've only just finished taking one statement, besides, she's busy preparing for tonight's bridge party.'

'Then you'd better catch her before she starts.'

Ten minutes later Daykin sat sipping tea from fine bone china brought in on a polished gallery tray by Mrs Morton. The cups and saucers were all unchipped and good quality, just not from the same tea set. Robert Morton's study was small and cluttered, a tiny room in a large Victorian vicarage. It was built as if it was an afterthought, the door half hidden under the giant ornate staircase. Morton sat at a battered mahogany desk which had never been the height of fashion but now with pieces of inlay missing, one leg supported by a thin paperback book and the top covered in piles of paper and coffee cup rings, it looked ready for a November bonfire.

Daykin sat opposite him on a hard upright chair, balancing his tea cup on his lap like a new boy being given the introductory talk in the headmaster's study.

'I've known Michael Hilliam for, let me see, when did I come to Camleigh?' Robert Morton tugged slowly and rhythmically at one of the cloth-covered buttons on the front of his cassock. It could have been habit or nerves, Daykin couldn't say.

'About five years. He owns an antique shop in Asquith. He's had it for about twenty years. He does quite well, imports a lot from France. He did, anyway,' said Morton. He fell into a troubled silence.

'Married?' prompted Daykin.

'Yes, I have been for twenty-five years.'

'No, Mr Hilliam. Was *he* married?'

'Divorced. I shouldn't say this, but he had a shrew of a wife. Always chasing him for money. It was a battleground of a marriage and the fighting didn't stop when they got divorced.'

The button tugging grew more furious. Nerves, definitely.

'Any children?'

'They were too busy arguing to conceive. It was a good thing really. You don't want children brought up in a house full of hate.'

'Any other relatives?'

'Not that I can think of. He did have a brother in Tadcaster. Or was that Tony Hammond, our other churchwarden. . . ?'

His voice trailed off and he stared through the window at the churchyard.

'Tony Hammond?' said Daykin gently.

'Oh yes,' said the vicar, his focus of attention coming back into the room, 'Tony and Michael were very friendly, Tony will miss him.'

'And where can we find Mr Hammond?'

'He's usually behind the bar at The Feathers at this time of day. He has not had a regular job since he came here; he doesn't need to work apparently, but he says he likes to do part-time bar work.'

'Since he came here?'

'Yes, about two years ago. He came from London or somewhere in that area. He said he preferred the solitude up here, and the clean air.'

'What can you tell me about him?'

Robert Morton smiled.

'Tony likes to think of himself as a cheeky Cockney sparrow, a jack the lad, but I'm not so sure that he is. He's certainly worked very hard for the church since he arrived here. He doesn't drink, smoke, take drugs, throw wild parties or get into fights. He lives very quietly, his only real friend is – was – Michael.'

'How often do you visit the church when there's not a service or a meeting?'

'Oh, let me see, it's so irregular it's hard to say, but about twice a week.'

'So no one would be expecting you this morning?'

'No, that's what's so awful; I only popped in to check everything was all right in the church.'

'Did anyone see you, or did you see anyone?'

'No.' The button tugging started again. 'Only Michael.'

'Who has keys to the church?'

'My two churchwardens and myself. Oh, and Mrs Sheppard as chairperson of the church fabric committee.'

'And the church is usually locked?'

'Yes, it's awful how it had been forced.'

Daykin closed his notebook.

'That's all for now Mr Morton. We may have some more questions later and in any event we'll need to take a formal statement from you. You're not planning on going away any time soon, are you?'

'Not on a country vicar's stipend, Inspector.'

Daykin walked towards Miss Murgatroyd's cottage and met Toby Peterson as he came out of the front door.

'What now?' asked Peterson.

'Sir,' said Daykin.

'I'm sorry?'

'Sir. You call me "sir". I don't care who your father is, what you call me behind my back or when you're off duty. At work it's "sir". Understood?'

'Yes, sir. And you can call me "Sergeant".'

'Don't push your luck, lad.'

'What does Miss Murgatroyd say about the people in the village?' he continued as they started to walk back towards the church.

'It's like a soap opera. Tony Hammond is the East End villain who's wormed his way into the church. The vicar is a bit scatterbrained, but has the soul of a saint, Michael Hilliam was weak and his wife, who attacked him with a breadknife more than once, was the wife from hell.'

'You chase the SOCO and get some idea when the post-mortem is, I'll meet you at the door of the church. I want to take a look at it.'

It took Toby Peterson thirty seconds to call the Scenes of Crimes Officer and be told that he was too busy right now, he'd call Peterson back. He snapped the phone shut and put it into his pocket. He looked round the church. By the pulpit Sergeant Carter was cramming evidence bags into a battered brown briefcase. Philip Carter had the air of a man who knew everyone's secrets and the look of a man who couldn't keep them. Peterson walked over to stand beside him.

'What's he like?'

Carter gave up the struggle with the briefcase and looked at the small pile of evidence bags still lying on the floor. He looked around for something else to put them into. Then he looked at Toby Peterson.

'I don't suppose you have a carrier bag on you, do you?'

Peterson shook his head.

Phil Carter started looking round the church again.

'Tom Daykin?' he said absently and smiled. 'He takes a lot of getting to know, but when he decides that he likes you, he likes you.'

'How do you know?'

'He starts calling you by your first name. And don't be fooled by his appearance. If you were in the middle of a pub quiz, a university debate or a bar brawl you'd want Tom Daykin on your side. He's got a mind like a computer and if we were both starving I wouldn't want to have to fight him for the last piece of bread.'

'A bar brawl?'

The smile had not left Philip Carter's face.

'A rugby player and not a man to be messed with in the middle of a scrum.' He looked hard at Toby Peterson, as if trying to decide just how much to tell the newcomer. 'If Tom

Daykin was a bitter man he'd have topped himself years ago. He was born with two priceless gifts, a great mind and a talent to play rugby. But in the space of six weeks fate took one away and sidelined the other.'

'What happened?'

Philip Carter leaned forward and lowered his voice, although no one was listening. 'About this time twenty-five years ago Tom Daykin had won a scholarship to Cambridge, was playing rugby for Yorkshire and was on the verge of the England team. Then he broke his ankle in a game he shouldn't have been playing in anyway, a charity match for God's sake! The ankle didn't mend properly, it's permanently weak and that put an end to his rugby career.'

'And Cambridge?'

'A few weeks earlier he had been so close that he had started to pack a suitcase. He was a brilliant scholar, good at most things, especially maths and history. Then his father died suddenly. He was a hill farmer and they found him one morning near the top of South Rise. He'd had a heart attack. It wasn't ever much of a farm, a few dozen sheep he grazed on the tops. Old man Daykin didn't do much more than scratch a living. Tom was the only boy in a family of four and he had to take care of them. He knew he wasn't a farmer, so he sold the farm, moved the family into a large crumbling house on the edge of the town and, as a stopgap to get some money, while he decided what to do, he joined the local police force. He's still here.'

'No ambition?'

Sergeant Carter looked at Toby Peterson with a steady stare.

'There are places, lad, where lack of ambition is a major problem. This isn't one of them.'

'Is he married?'

'Was.'

'Divorced?'

'Because divorce goes with the job? No, Jenny Daykin died two years ago now.'

Toby Peterson mentally pictured Jenny Daykin. A plump, badly dressed woman in an apron. Prematurely grey hair tied in a bun. She had bad teeth and baked cakes for the Women's Institute.

'What was she like?' he asked, just to see if reality matched the image.

'Jenny? She was the sort of girl every man wants to take home and every mother dreams that he does. She was beautiful and I don't mean just physically. Everyone, men and women, loved her. She was kind, loyal and understanding. When she married Tom Daykin they were the only ones for thirty miles around who weren't surprised. She broke any number of hearts' – he paused for a second – 'and I'm not sure mine wasn't one of them.'

'What happened to her?'

'Cancer. The worst kind. From the moment she broke the news to Tom to leaving him was just three months. I don't think it gave him time to grieve. The day after he buried her he was back at the station, working all hours. Then the drinking started.'

'Drinking?'

'Brandy of all things. I'd never seen him touch a drop before Jenny died.'

'Does he still drink now?'

'He stopped as quickly as he started, as if he had to get something out of his system. The answer is yes, he still has the odd pint or glass of wine, but he hasn't touched the hard stuff for about eighteen months.'

'So he's not an alcoholic?'

'Enough questions.'

Whoever had forced the church door had done a thorough job. It was an old oak door but it was not as old as it looked. It was the sort of door that was mass produced a century ago as the ideal of a medieval door. The doorway was a Norman arch and the door fitted snugly into it. It was hung on three heavy hinges, each with a large rusting hinge strap screwed into the wood, running half way across the door. There were heavy cross members round the outline of the door and across it, in line with the huge straps. Black rectangular bolts, used to hold the door together when knights rode chargers but by the early twentieth century just cosmetic, studded the door in a grid pattern. A circular metal handle lifted the latch and below it the only real functional item, a huge black box encasing the formidable lock. The wood itself, pale oak, now the colour of mahogany after years of coats of varnish, had been the picture of a country church door, the sort of door that tourists photographed. That was, until someone had taken a crowbar to it.

Pale against the dark outer surface, large chunks of unvarnished wood had been exposed by two or three brutal pulls on a large crowbar that had shattered the woodwork and left the lock bent at an odd angle, like a broken limb. Pieces of wood lay on the floor by the doorway. Daykin bent down to look at the damage.

He felt, rather than heard, Toby Peterson walking up behind him along the cobbled pathway from the back door of the church.

'The SOCO's got some bits and pieces for you, sir, and the post-mortem will be at seven this evening.'

'OK,' said Daykin rising to his feet and brushing dirt from the knees of his trousers, 'then we've got time to see Mr Hammond.'

CHAPTER FIVE

THE High Street sliced through the centre of Camleigh, clean and straight as a butcher's knife cut. What few shops and offices there were in the village stood in the neat rows of buildings either side of the road, separated from it by a narrow strip of grass. On one side, at the centre of the row, and standing back from the other buildings, was The Feathers public house. It was the largest building on the High Street, the only one with three storeys. It served bed and breakfast, had four bedrooms and three crowns from the English tourist board. The bedrooms, all on the top floor, were kept clean and tidy, although no one could remember anyone stopping at the village unexpectedly and asking to be put up for the night.

As Daykin walked across the small car-park in front of the pub, the wind had picked up and the sign swung noisily and dangerously on hinges that hadn't seen oil for years. He climbed the three concrete steps and walked through a front door which was flanked by stone columns supporting a pitched canopy that were some long forgotten builder's idea of a Grecian portico.

Inside the entrance two multiple windowed doors were held open on catches and through them two identical newly painted doors labelled 'lounge' and 'snug' led to the left and right. Knowing what little he did about Tony Hammond, Daykin thought he would prefer the larger audience of the lounge bar and without a word to Toby Peterson who was following him, he opened the door and stepped into the lounge bar. He stepped into a time warp.

The room, twice as long as it was wide, stretched to the back of the building, dog legging to the right at the far end to the back entrance to the snug bar. Running almost full length of the room to his right was a bar topped with a row of porcelain beer handles, cracked and yellowed with age. Along the left wall was a line of tables in front of damask-covered benches backing on to the wall with pairs of matching stools on the other side of each table. The flock-wallpapered walls, hung with mirrors advertising breweries and pictures of country life, and ceiling had all seen better days and the carpet, although nearly new, was woven in an old fashioned floral pattern. The view Daykin saw as he glanced round the room could not have changed for sixty years.

There were two men behind the bar, one an oldish man with greasy grey hair and nicotine-stained fingers. The other wore a dark green open-necked silk shirt, the sleeves rolled up just enough to show the expensive gold watch on his left wrist. He stared expectantly at them as they came into the room and walked to the bar.

'What can I do for you, gents?' he asked, his hand already moving towards the row of pint glasses just below the bar.

'Tony Hammond?' asked Daykin.

The hand stopped and the eyes narrowed slightly.

'Who wants to know?'

Daykin pushed his warrant card across the bar.

'I'm sure you've heard about the murder at the church this

morning.' said Daykin, who knew that in a village all gossip was started and amplified in the pub. 'Can we talk?'

Tony Hammond looked at the warrant card, then at Daykin.

'Why me?'

'It's just routine, Mr Hammond,' said Daykin, putting the card back in his pocket. 'A bit of background, that's all.'

He looked round the room again.

'Anywhere we can speak in private?'

The room was quiet, just two small groups of men sitting silently at tables near the door, concentrating on the serious business of drinking beer. Tony Hammond pointed to a table in the corner by the back wall.

When they were seated and Toby Peterson had put his open notebook on the table, Hammond said again, 'Why me? Mike was my best friend up here.'

'That's why we want to talk to you.' said Daykin quietly, 'just a few questions about Mr Hilliam's daily routine and anything else that you could tell us about him.'

'Let's see. Most days he worked normal shop hours at the antiques business, except, of course, when he was off buying for the shop.'

'Did he go away often?'

'About once every two months.'

'How long was he away?'

'It varied, often only two or three days, sometimes up to seven.'

'Seems a long time to be away from the shop. Where did he go?'

'Oh, you know, the usual auctions. He used to say the business is not what it was, you can't get the bargains now that these bloody television programmes have made everyone an antiques expert.'

'Days off?'

'He closed Sundays and had a half day Wednesday, otherwise he didn't have any time off.'

'Staff?'

'No one regular. Mrs Potterton would come in to man the shop when he was away buying. And he always took the first two weeks in August as his holiday.'

'So, nothing unusual in his life,' said Daykin. 'Do you know any reason why anyone would want to kill him?'

'If you put a hundred people in a room and asked someone to choose who would get murdered, poor old Mike would be their hundredth choice.'

'Thank you, Mr Hammond,' said Daykin, nodding again to Toby Peterson to put his notebook away. 'We're sorry to have interrupted your day, you've been very helpful.'

As they walked out of the pub, Peterson said, 'Anything useful in that, sir?'

'One thing Tony Hammond said that is the absolute truth, there's something strange about Michael Hilliam. People like him don't get murdered. There must be a lot about him we don't know. While we wait for the pathologist and the SOCO to tell us something, let's take a look at his house and shop.'

CHAPTER SIX

IN twenty years of marriage Mark Jarvis had had five affairs. He didn't see himself as a serial adulterer, just a man who needed a bit of spice with the bland dish of his marriage. His domestic sex life, never sexual Olympics even when they were newly married, had long ago sunk into an indifferent routine. He was always very careful, although he sometimes thought that his wife might suspect, but turned a blind eye to his infidelity.

Each affair had started the same way. Usually a woman he worked with. A few conversations, inviting her for a drink, then a meal. He could be very persuasive and after a lot of attention, flowers and champagne he would tell his wife that he had to go to a weekend conference and the affair would become serious.

Now his attention had turned to that tall, attractive and interesting woman, Paula Sykes.

He took out the buff file from his desk drawer and opened it. It was a photocopy of her personnel file, he'd had it couriered from headquarters, a minor disciplinary matter he had told them. What was the point of rank if you couldn't pull it? No point in starting an affair and discovering she had skeletons in her closet. He read the file again, for the fourth time.

She was in her thirties, had never been married and came from a large family of four girls and three boys. A minor public school near Guildford, one of those universities that used to be technical colleges, studying chemistry. She had an interest in pharmaceuticals and an ambition to work in the research laboratories of one of the large drugs companies. The file didn't say why, but instead she had taken a short service commission in the army. She had blotted her copybook there, but at least she had been discreet and that, right now, was what was important.

He scoured the pages, looking for what might be a problem if he started an affair and, more important, when he finished it. He always finished them before they got serious enough to threaten his career.

There were no potential problems, just an attractive woman, junior to him in rank, years and experience with no romantic ties or psychological problems. Just about ideal. Short in height and not stunningly attractive, Mark Jarvis was convinced that the force of his personality could charm any woman into bed. He decided that the assault on Paula Sykes's chastity would start tomorrow morning.

There had been a set of keys in Michael Hilliam's jacket pocket when he died and Daykin used them to unlock the door of his house. There was no surprise that it was full of antiques. An ornate mahogany grandfather clock stood just inside the front door, its top nearly touching the low ceiling. The noise of the slow, constant rhythmic swing of the pendulum was the only sound in the house. It reminded Daykin of the church where the owner of this house had died.

'You take upstairs, I'll look round down here,' said Daykin

as he gently pushed open the inner door to a short hallway.

Toby Peterson had brought two pairs of latex gloves from the car and handed one pair to Daykin. They both pulled them on wordlessly and Peterson climbed the stairs slowly, looking intently at each step as he climbed it. Daykin watched him and shook his head.

'Have you got a thing about footprints, lad?'

Toby Peterson stopped, looked at him, then walked up the rest of the stairs.

Daykin started with the living-room, the first door opening off the hall. The room was almost an exact square, overcrowded with furniture like an old fashioned parlour. The sofa, occasional chairs, plant stands, chest of drawers and piano were all antique, so were the vases and plates that stood on them. The room was clean, tidy and neat. Too neat; more like a museum than a place where someone lived. It was the room of an obsessive man. Daykin opened a few drawers. The contents were stacked in ordered rows, nothing like the drawers in Daykin's home or office. He moved to the next room.

The dining-room had a large bay window that opened on to the back of the house. At the end of the garden, just the other side of a low red brick wall, was the churchyard, empty and silent now that Trevor Wilkins had finished digging the grave and had moved on to another church. This room was more Georgian than Victorian, sparsely furnished with an oval dining-table surrounded by four wheatsheaf backed chairs and, against the far wall, a sideboard. Daykin opened the cupboard doors and drawers of the sideboard. More possessions in neat, regimented military lines.

He was halfway through the cupboards in the kitchen when he heard Toby Peterson's footsteps on the stairs.

Peterson came into the kitchen.

'Anything?' asked Daykin.

'No surprises, nothing out of the ordinary.'

'Everything where it should be?'

Peterson nodded, looking at the open cupboards full of rows of stacked crockery and groceries.

'Got your mobile?' asked Daykin.

Toby Peterson pulled it from his jacket pocket to show him.

'Call the station. Get six or seven officers over here as a search team. Go through this place from attic to cellar. Make a note of anything out of the ordinary. Phil Carter will be the Exhibits Officer.'

'Aren't you going to be here, sir?'

'I'll take a look at his shop, it can't be very big and I can do that on my own.'

Daykin drove the back way to Asquith, taking the narrow winding road to the top of Butterbridge Hill where there was a hardstanding. He parked his car on it, got out and leant against the side of the vehicle. He took a large paisley handkerchief from his pocket, removed his glasses and slowly polished the lenses in tiny circular movements, all the time staring at the rolling pattern of fields in the valley below him. He stood like that, deep in thought, for nearly twenty minutes.

Suddenly coming to his senses and realizing that his hands were aching with the constant polishing, he put the glasses back on his face, got back into the car and drove down the hill towards the town.

Michael Hilliam's shop stood on the corner of the main street and a dirt road that led to the cattle market. There was a gravel car-park directly across the street, so Daykin parked the car facing the shop and sat examining the building through the windscreen, running his hand through his wiry, untidy hair.

When it was built about ninety years earlier, no one would think of opening an antique shop in a small market town. The shop had been occupied most of its life by a butcher, grocer, or fishmonger. Now, the terrazzo floor in the entranceway to the central door, the leaded windows that ran along the top of the main display windows and the ornate woodwork made it appear to have been designed to be a shop for the sale of antiques.

Unlike many of the shops on the street, it was well maintained. The dark-green paintwork was fresh and unchipped, the two large windows running at right angles to each other away from the doorway, were clean and well stocked with furniture and the door itself boasted a brass handle and letterbox which gleamed in the faint afternoon sunlight. Identical neatly painted signs in art deco lettering ran over the top of both windows 'M. Hilliam. Purveyor of Fine Antiques.' A bit pompous for Daykin's liking, but what did he know?

As Daykin looked at the building one thing was very odd. It was the security. There were large alarm boxes on both exterior walls, grilles inside the display window and, when he looked carefully, Daykin could see three separate keyholes in a neat line down the right side of the door. He pulled the bunch of keys he had used to open the house out of his trouser pocket and examined it. On a ring with a leather Gucci fob there were six keys. Daykin had used one of the keys to open the front door of the house and he guessed that two others were for the back door and the garage. The other three must be for the shop. Daykin did not know much about keys, but he knew the look of an expensive security key and these three, made by different companies, were top-of-therange keys, designed for serious locks.

He put his finger through the centre of the key ring and swung it gently from side to side while he looked at the late Mr Hilliam's shop. There was a problem. He was sure that the keys on the ring fitted the locks, but when he opened the door the alarm would go off and he hadn't a clue how to stop it. He looked up and down the High Street and smiled to himself. At the far end, next to the newsagent, was a shop front with a sign that read 'Pearson and Collins, Estate Agents and Property Management'. If they managed the antiques shop, problem solved. He got out of the car and the dog jumped out as he opened the door. They looked at each other and the dog stared him out from behind a veil of white hair.

'Behave yourself, Royston,' said Daykin, taking the lead out of his pocket.

When he stepped through the door of the estate agents he had his warrant card ready. It was an open plan office with six identical modern desks, each dominated by a computer screen and keyboard. Three of the desks were occupied and he walked to the nearest one where a middle-aged man stopped typing with two fingers and watched him approach. Daykin flashed his warrant card and the salesman's welcoming smile that had just lit up went out instantly.

'Do you manage Hilliam's antique shop?' asked Daykin.

Realizing that he might be a witness, not a suspect, the smile returned and he held out his hand.

'We do.' He shook hands. 'Stuart Pearson, Senior Partner.'

'Do you know the code to deactivate the alarm at the shop?'

'Funny you should say that. I know that we do, because we had the devil of a job persuading Mr Hilliam to give it to us.'

He got up, strolled to a bank of filing cabinets and opened one of the drawers.

'Yes, here it is,' he said over his shoulder, as he read a file he had pulled out of the drawer. 'As I said to him, the lease gives us the power to enter the premises even if the tenant is not there, to check on the building. When we noticed that Mr Hilliam had installed an alarm, I rang him and asked him for the code. He point blank refused. He said there was no point in an alarm if every Tom, Dick and Harry knew the code. Eventually, we came to a compromise. He let us have the code and we guaranteed that no one outside this office would be given it and that we would not enter the shop unless he was there, except in an emergency.

'So you see, Inspector,' he continued, 'if I give you the code. I'm going to get some flack from Mr Hilliam.'

'No you won't, Mr Pearson. I'm afraid he's dead.'

'Good God. I didn't particularly like him, but I wouldn't wish him dead.' Then the professionalism took over. 'I suppose we'll have to think about re-letting.'

'Now,' said Pearson. looking round the office, 'where did I put the keys to the shop?'

'Don't worry,' said Daykin 'I have Mr Hilliam's set.'

'Well, I suppose I'd better come with you, to check on the shop.' The temptation to re-let immediately was too strong.

'I think you'll find that checking on the shop is my job,' said Daykin.

'Yes, of course, but the alarm plays up sometimes. I know how to handle it,' said Stuart Pearson as forcefully as he could. He tucked the file under his arm to show Daykin that he wasn't going to give away the alarm code easily.

As they walked to the shop Daykin asked some routine questions.

'How long did Mr Hilliam have the shop?'

'About twenty years.'

'Good tenant?'

'Yes. He paid his rent on the dot on the first working day of the month and always kept the shop immaculate, both inside and out.'

'Was business good?'

'I really don't know. I assume so. He didn't complain about it and, believe me, if complaining was money he'd be a very wealthy man.'

They arrived at the door of the shop and Daykin passed Stuart Pearson the keys, he appeared to want to be in charge. Pearson opened each lock in turn.

'Let's just hope he hasn't bought a vicious dog as well,' said Daykin.

'I don't think so,' replied Pearson as he turned the last lock, 'he wasn't a dog sort of a person.'

But he opened the door very slowly, just in case, and only moved quickly when the alarm warning siren began to wail. He half ran to a control panel under the stairs and tapped in four digits. The alarm control box went silent.

Daykin followed him into the shop. If the exterior was well cared for, the interior was immaculate. The walls were newly decorated in pastel shades, the whitewood shone brilliantly and the carpet was expensive and freshly vacuumed. It was, like the house, the rooms of an obsessive man. In one of the windows were four carved dining chairs. They stood like soldiers on parade, their feet in a ruler straight line and each chair exactly the sane distance from its neighbours. Around the room were pieces of antique furniture of different ages and designs. Uniformly, they were all clean and polished. Daykin guessed that dust wouldn't dare settle in this room.

'Is there an office?' he asked.

'I suppose so, but I've hardly been in here since he opened.'

Daykin walked to the back of the room, towards and
through the only other door. At the other side of it was an
office and a small kitchen, neatly divided by emulsioned
walls.

'The work looks new,' said Daykin.

'It's not, it was done about five years after he moved in;
fifteen years ago. It must have been decorated recently. He
was always calling the decorators in.'

'But he only called the builders in once?'

'Not even that. He did the building work himself. I don't
know if he had any training' – he leant to one side to look
along the line of the wall with a professional eye – 'but he did
a good job.'

Daykin walked passed Stuart Pearson into the office.
Against the left hand wall was an old desk, which must have
been used regularly, but it had the same showroom appearance as the furniture in the main room. To its right stood an
ancient but solid safe, polished brass fittings against dark
green paint, just like the front door of the shop.

'Do you have a key to the safe?' he asked, staring at the
keyhole.

'Are you joking? It took me all my time to get a set of shop
keys out of him.'

Daykin pulled casually at one of the desk drawers. To his
surprise, it opened.

'Shouldn't you have a warrant, or something?' asked Stuart
Pearson.

'I don't think Mr Hilliam is going to complain.' said
Daykin, starting to run his hands through the neat rows of
documents.

In the third drawer he pulled out a key and held it up, staring at it quizzically.

'What's the problem?' asked Pearson.

'Why,' replied Daykin, kneeling down in front of the safe and inserting the key into the lock, 'would you go to the trouble of having a safe and then leave the key in an unlocked drawer next to it?'

There was no answer as the key turned with a metallic clunk, the massive locking bars moving back flush with the edge of the door. Daykin swung the heavy door open. They both stared into the dark interior of the safe, Stuart Pearson moving so that he could look over Daykin's shoulder. If either of them expected to see anything interesting, they were disappointed. The safe was practically empty. On its floor were only two things: a passport and a bundle of bank notes. Daykin lifted the passport out and examined it. The photograph was as bad as passport photographs are, but there was no mistaking Michael Hilliam's face staring back at him, a grim expression in full colour. The typed personal details were all correct, so the passport was genuine, Mr Hilliam was not leading the double life of a spy. Daykin leant forward with a small involuntary grunt and picked up the bundle of notes. He flipped through them. Held together with a narrow rubber band, they were a selection of Euro notes that, he guessed, amounted to nine or ten thousand. He looked up at Stuart Pearson.

'Why would a small-time antique dealer want thousands of pounds in Euros in his office safe?'

'France.'

'Sorry?'

'France. It's where he bought a lot of his antiques. He went across there four or five times a year. I suppose cash is as persuasive there as it is anywhere. It's his stock in trade.'

'Why France?'

'I asked him the same question. He said it was cheap. He was right, I have a friend in antiques in Manchester and he says that if you are prepared to put in the time and the miles, you can get some real bargains in the French antiques markets.'

'His French must have been better than average.'

'It was. I once heard him on the telephone to France.'

Daykin took a few paces and looked round the main showroom. Rich carpet, batteries of spotlights, freshly decorated walls and expensive antiques.

'I've seen enough for now.' said Daykin making a few notes in his notebook, 'but I'll probably be back for a thorough look round.'

He stood outside the shop and watched Stuart Pearson set the alarm and lock the front door.

'I'll take the keys.' he said, as Stuart Pearson moved to put them in his pocket.

As Pearson walked back to his office, Daykin patted his pockets, searching for his mobile telephone. Jarvis had eventually forced him to accept a mobile telephone. That was eight months ago and he still had not got used to it. He slowly stopped patting his pockets as it dawned on him that he had left it on his desk, plugged into the charger. He looked up and down the street. At the other end, nearly opposite where he had parked the car, was a telephone box. With a sigh he set off to walk to it. Before he got to it, it had started to rain.

The telephone box was like a thousand others, red metalwork, concrete floor, a door and two walls of multiple small square windows, some of them missing. He told the dog to wait outside, it didn't mind the rain. He picked up the telephone and dialled Toby Peterson's mobile number. Peterson answered almost immediately.

'How's it going?' asked Daykin.

'The search team say they'll be finished in about an hour.'

'Anything interesting?'

'Nothing out of the ordinary. Except. . . .'

'Except?'

'Well, forget all the antiques, he was an antique dealer after all, it's just that he lived well.'

'This is like wading through treacle,' said Daykin, 'spit it out.'

'His television and sound system, state of the art and top of the line. His larder, stocked from a very exclusive delicatessen, four bottles of champagne in the fridge and a wardrobe full of designer clothes and half-a-dozen suits made by the most expensive tailor in Harrogate.'

'How do you know he's the most expensive tailor in Harrogate?'

'It's where my father buys his suits.'

Daykin looked at himself in the small mirror above the telephone and grimaced. He wished he hadn't asked.

'I'll come over there, see you in about thirty minutes.'

He put the telephone down. He hated telephones.

Daykin drove hack to Camleigh on the main roads and was at the house within twenty minutes. Toby Peterson must have seen him arrive, he met him at the front door.

'The search team are finishing off the bedrooms upstairs,' he said.

Daykin walked through the door, along the short hallway and into the living-room. Kneeling by a large cardboard box filled with items sealed in clear plastic bags was the familiar back of an overweight middle-aged man dressed in crumpled flannel trousers and a blazer. He was writing a list of items into an exhibits log.

'Anything to make us sit up and take notice, Phil?'

The other man looked up.

'Hello, Tom.' He got slowly to his feet, an act that took all his concentration and effort. Although it was cool in the room, he was sweating.

'Nothing out of the ordinary. We bagged his diaries and any other documents, the kitchen knives, just in case they show anything, his photo albums and videos, his answering machine and that's about it.'

'Forensics?'

'There's a team coming' – he looked at his watch – 'in two hours. They'll give the place the once over, but nobody expects that they'll find anything.'

'Well,' said Daykin, 'let's head back to the station and see what we can do there.'

On the way back to the station Toby Peterson tried to make conversation.

'What do you make of Superintendent Jarvis, sir?'

'Jarvis? He can be a bit anal, but deep down he's a good policeman and, unless it would damage him, he'd back you if you got yourself into trouble.'

'And Chief Inspector Sykes?'

'Off the record?'

'Of course.'

'She's driven.'

'Driven?'

'It's a name selfish, obsessive people have invented to describe themselves. It sounds better.'

'But they both want a quick solution to this murder; do you have any suspects?'

'In the mortuary there's a churchwarden who looks like he's been crucified in his own church late at night. Supects? It could be a religious fanatic and we may have to wait until he kills again. In the meantime, we've only seen the vicar and Miss Murgatroyd. Either of them have the look of a psychopath?'

Toby Peterson fell back into silence.

CHAPTER SEVEN

DAYKIN walked to his office and settled the dog on the rug in the corner. Then he noticed the pink sheet of paper in the middle of the desk. Jarvis always used pink paper for memos. He picked it up and read it. The Superintendent wanted a progress report. Daykin screwed up the memo and threw it in the wastepaper basket. The dog looked up at the noise.

'Not now, Royston,' said Daykin. He needed to see Jarvis anyway so he walked towards the Superintendent's office. Jarvis was standing in the corridor.

'We need an incident room.' Daykin said.

'We don't have the space.'

'What about a Portakabin in the car-park?'

Jarvis stroked his chin. He could make this appear to the Assistant Chief Constable to be his idea.

'I'll get Sergeant Carter to make the arrangements,' he said, 'only a small Portakabin, mind you.'

Daykin nodded, but Superintendent Jarvis had already turned his back and was walking away into the building.

It was the shine from the highly polished buttons he noticed first as Chief Inspector Sykes, immaculately uniformed as usual, came towards them from the far end of the corridor. He put his head down and hoped that they would pass each other without speaking.

'Inspector,' said Sykes from ten feet away, 'I hear that you've got a murder.'

'That's right, ma'am, it's keeping us very busy,' said Daykin, keeping his head down and his pace up.

But Paula Sykes wasn't going to be side-stepped so easily. She stopped directly in front of Daykin, blocking his path. This was becoming a habit.

'I'm told its one of the churchwardens.'

'That's right, ma'am,' said Daykin, wondering where the conversation was going.

'Which one?'

'Michael Hilliam, the senior warden,' said Daykin, although Chief Inspector Sykes wouldn't know either warden from Adam.

'Any progress?'

'It's early days yet, ma'am. As soon as we come up with something I'll let you know.'

'Be sure that you do. I take it, then, that you have no suspects?'

'Not as yet, ma'am,' said Daykin, 'what's your interest?'

'I came here from a Birmingham city centre station, if there wasn't a murder every week, it seemed as if there was. I have ten times more experience in investigating murders than all the officers in this station put together. You need my help.'

'I'll bear that in mind.'

'And what's this about stigmata?'

'It wasn't stigmata, it was just made to look like it.'

'I've seen more than my share of religious fanatics; you really do need my help.'

'I'll bear that in mind too.'

Paula Sykes had made her point, she walked round Daykin and up the corridor.

'Where have you been, sir?' asked Toby Peterson when Daykin found him in the charge office.

'Let's have a cup of tea,' replied Daykin.

'Your dad's not going to want a daily report as well, is he?' asked Daykin, when he finally had a mug of hot tea on the beer mat on his desk.

'If he does, he'll probably ask me over dinner.'

'Good. But here's the first lesson of being a detective. Your superiors don't need to know everything, they only end up wanting to get involved.'

'What can we do now?' asked Peterson.

'These days, a lot of this job is down to the specialists. The pathologist, forensic laboratory. Scenes of Crimes Officers or Crime Scene Investigators as they like to call themselves now, but there is one thing we do better than any of them.'

'What?'

'Finding out about the victim.'

CHAPTER EIGHT

I<small>T</small> wasn't much. Six cardboard boxes on the floor of Daykin's office, filled with plastic bags. Inside some of the bags were piles of documents, others bulging with larger, solid objects. Each bag was tied with a bright yellow label with a hand-written list of its contents. Daykin looked through the exhibits book which lay on his desk.

'Right,' he said finally, staring at the boxes the search team had taken from Michael Hilliam's house, 'let's go.'

'What are we looking for?' asked Toby Peterson.

'Anything unusual. If you find anything, put it to one side.'

For the next three hours they worked their way through the boxes. It was hard work and, by the time they had finished, Daykin had in front of him a set of MOT certificates, in date order and neatly stapled together, and a hotel bill. Toby Peterson had nothing.

'What have you got, sir?' Toby Peterson asked, hopefully.

Daykin looked at his watch. He was tired, physically and emotionally.

'Nothing that can't wait until tomorrow.'

Daykin drove home, parked the car outside his house and

opened the front door. He shut it behind him and leant his back against it, closing his eyes tightly and holding his breath. This was always the worst part of the day, when he came home and she wasn't there. He missed everything about her, the smell of her, the sound of her singing, usually off key, the sight of her face, always smiling, just her being there. When she died they told him that the pain would ease and sometimes it did, but never now, never at the doorway of this house. He should have moved, cut the traces of the memories, but moving house would somehow have distanced him from her spirit, so he stayed here and faced some pain, but a lot of comfort in the possessions they had shared together.

Someone who didn't know him well and didn't know he could cook, had given him a microwave just after Jenny's death. He took some seafood filling he had made last week from the freezer and defrosted it in the microwave, the only reason he ever used it. Then he made some pancake batter and spread it in thin discs with a spatula, the way the Belgians do, on a hot griddle. He filled the pancakes with the seafood and ate at the old wooden kitchen table that Jenny had scrubbed with bleach every day so that it was almost white. He idly thumbed through the evening's television programmes. As usual there were only a couple he half wanted to watch, so he washed up, made himself a cup of tea and took it with him to bed. If he was lucky he would be asleep by nine and only wake up four or five times in the night.

CHAPTER NINE

THE following morning dawned a dour grey day. The low clouds hung in a level seamless sheet over the valleys and settled themselves ominously on the hilltops. The sun must have been above them somewhere, but it didn't have a chance of shining through the uniform dark mass. Daykin looked up at the clouds as he drove to the station. There would be rain, but maybe not until later in the day.

To the north of the town, beyond the road that ran down the valley, the ground rose steeply through sparse woodland to high heather covered moorland. From the narrow path that ran along the top of the moors a figure in a heavy wax jacket and jeans tucked into thick socks inside brown walking boots looked down at the police station.

Chief Inspector Paula Sykes missed the frantic pace and noise of a large city centre, but the countryside had its advantages. Up here on the Dales on her own gave her the time and space to think. It was tranquil on the moors, even when the wind howled and the rain lashed horizontally. She thought about her job and her past. She came up here on her days off every time her shifts let her get away from work before it was dark.

Her gaze shifted back to the moorland and she stood there motionless, breathing the cold clear air deeply into her lungs. Then she looked at her watch. She had a Burmese cat who spent most of his time prowling the streets of Shapford but came home for food at regular times, as if he could read a clock. He would be scratching at the door in fifteen minutes. Just time to call in at the station for a magazine she had left on her desk, then home before the cat. A path ran at right-angles to the one she was on, snaking down towards the town. She turned and strode towards it.

She was walking down the corridor with the magazine tucked under her arm when Superintendnt Jarvis caught up with her and took hold of her elbow. It was a small intimate gesture she had never seen from him before.

'Chief Inspector,' he began smoothly, 'I wonder if we know each other well enough for me to ask a favour?'

'What can I do for you, sir?'

'You can help me solve a small problem. You see, I have been invited to dinner by the Assistant Chief Constable to discuss staffing and a number of other station issues.'

'Yes, sir?'

'He'll be bringing his wife and will expect me to have someone with me, four at the table will be far more comfortable than three.'

'What about your wife?'

'The ACC met his wife in the force, so there will he a lot of talk about the job and she would be bored to death. Anyway, she's away visiting her mother in St Helens.'

'And you want me to go with you?'

'A free meal, a chance to talk to the ACC face to face and my undying gratitude. Surely, you can't refuse?'

She didn't say anything for ten seconds and he was afraid

he'd got the sales pitch wrong.

'It would be a pleasure, sir.'

'Excellent.' he said, trying not to sound too enthusiastic, 'I'm afraid there is one other thing.'

'Sir?'

'Short notice. It's tonight.'

'That's all right, sir. I'm on early shift.'

Mark Jarvis knew that, he'd checked the rotas on his computer.

'Great, I'll pick you up at about seven-thirty.'

'What should I wear?'

'I'm sure you have a little black number in your wardrobe, that will be fine.'

'Seven-thirty, then, sir.'

'I look forward to it.'

They walked off in opposite directions along the corridor. They were both smiling, but for different reasons.

Toby Peterson was waiting for Daykin in his office.

'Coffee, sir?' asked Peterson.

Daykin nodded and motioned to the dog to lie down in the corner of the room. He must have taken it for a walk earlier. Toby Peterson could see the dew in the long hairs on its legs and the room smelt of damp wool. He walked out and came back with two mugs of instant coffee. Daykin hated instant coffee, but said nothing.

'I hope you don't mind, I've looked through those papers you pulled out last night. What's so interesting about them?' said Peterson, sipping his coffee.

Daykin took a tentative sip from his own mug. Toby Peterson had put at least two sugars in the coffee and Daykin didn't take sugar. Two sugars in instant coffee. He put the mug to one side and picked up the MOT certificates.

'This bundle are all the certificates since the Transit was three years old. The mileage goes up by about ten thousand a year.'

'So?'

'Tony Hammond said that he went to France five or six times a year. That's a round trip of about seventeen hundred miles. Six times is ten thousand two hundred. Add trips to the auctions, deliveries and travelling to and from work six times a week, that's probably another five thousand. Why was the van only doing ten thousand a year?'

'He had another van?'

'He was meticulous, if he'd had another van we would have seen some evidence of it.'

'And this,' he said, picking up the other document, 'is a hotel bill found in the lining of one of his suits. It's made out to Jonathan Lister who stayed at a hotel, The Château des Ollières in Nice last February for four days where he ran up a bill,' he mentally calculated euros into pounds, 'of about a thousand quid. I've seen a laptop on your desk, bring it in here, will you?'

Two minutes later Peterson opened the lid of a slim silver laptop computer and typed in his password. The screensaver, a picture of a red Ferrari, appeared on the screen.

'Your car?' said Daykin.

'I wish.'

'Start with the Château des Ollières, see if they've got a website.'

The Ferrari was replaced by colour photographs of an opulent hotel, rich brocade curtains, deep pile carpets and French Empire furniture.

'Looks like Michael Hilliam's sort of place,' said Daykin. 'Now let's see if we can contact the local police.'

'Don't we have an international directory?'

'Have you met Mavis?'

'Good point.'

Toby Peterson started typing.

'I'll try a search engine,' he said and studied the screen.

'Yep, here they are, telephone and fax numbers.'

'Put them on the speakerphone.'

It took thirty seconds for Toby Peterson to know that his GCSE French would get him nowhere. He was speaking to a woman who couldn't, or wouldn't, speak English. His frustration was nearing boiling point, he looked over his shoulder at Daykin, looking for help and knowing that he wouldn't get any. Daykin leaned forward and started speaking in fluent French to the woman, whose attitude changed instantly. He asked for the duty inspector and while they waited Daykin shrugged his shoulders.

'Six months waiting tables in Auxerre before I was due to go to university.'

'Inspector Lebrun,' said a voice from the loudspeaker on the phone.

Daykin explained that he needed some questions asked about a man called Jonathan Lister who stayed at the Château des Ollières hotel and that he would fax a photograph to see if the staff could identify the man. The inspector said that he would send a couple of men round to the hotel and would call Daykin when they came back.

Now there was nothing to do but wait.

Daykin looked at a grease spot on his lapel and rubbed it with his thumbnail. It didn't go away. He looked at the dog lying in the corner of the office. He was worried about the cut in its back paw; it wouldn't heal and he would have to call the vet. He drummed his fingers on the desktop whilst Toby

Peterson idly moved the cursor round the computer screen in small patterns.

'Does your father give you a hard time?' asked Daykin eventually. It was a stupid question, asked out of boredom.

'Not really, my brother got the worst of it when we were growing up.'

'How many brothers do you have?'

'Only the one. You?'

'No brothers. Three sisters, all married.'

'They live locally?'

'Yes, we're not a family who stray very far. That means that I see my five nephews and four nieces pretty often and spoil them rotten.'

Toby Peterson had no nephews or nieces so the conversation juddered to a halt again. After fifteen minutes Daykin left a message with Mavis to call him on his mobile if an inspector from France rang and they went for a coffee in the town. They had been back for half an hour when the phone on Daykin's desk rang. Toby Peterson got to it first and switched it to speakerphone, although he would only catch a fraction of the conversation.

'Your Jonathan Lister, he's a strange man,' said Lebrun, 'he stayed at the hotel regularly and spent a lot of money on clothes, restaurants and the casinos. But he was always alone and kept to himself.'

There was a pause, as if the inspector was reading some notes.

'He had breakfast in his room but he never ate dinner at the hotel. Only the chambermaid, a woman called Yvette Benastre, saw him more than once. She says that the photgraph you sent is not him.'

'Is she sure?'

'Yes, this man was younger, his hair was darker and he wore glasses. She remembers him because he tipped so well. That's another thing, he paid for everything, even the hotel bill, in cash.'

'Anything else you can tell us?'

'Only this, Madame Benastre saw plane ticket stubs in his wastepaper basket on several occasions, they were always planes from Paris.'

'So he flew from Paris to Nice. What do you think he was doing in Paris, Inspector?'

'Search me, but I'll tell you what I'll do. I have a cousin in The Sûreté, Sergent Dupont, I've got the date your man last made the trip from Paris to Nice. I'll ask him to see what he can find out about Mr Lister.'

One of Mark Jarvis's obsessions was punctuality. The wheels of his car stopped at the kerb in front of Paula Sykes's house at exactly 7.30. As usual, he had been careful, not putting on the expensive cologne until after he left home.

When she came to the door Paula Sykes was wearing a plain black dress with a burgundy silk stole round her shoulders. She had washed and conditioned her hair and she wore it down, so that it fell to the nape of her neck and the shoulder-straps of her dress. Jarvis noticed with some pleasure that she had taken her time in applying make-up. The only thing that spoilt her appearance for him was that she was, for the first time since he had met her, wearing high heels. It made her five inches taller than him.

'I never thought I'd say this when I joined the police force,' he said, 'but, Chief Inspector, you look stunning.'

She smiled that lop-sided smile that he had grown to like.

They walked to his car and he opened the door for her,

watching her swing those long legs into the passenger footwell before he closed it.

'I'm really sorry about this.' he said as he got into the driver's seat, 'change of plan, the ACC can't make it, his wife is suffering a migraine.'

'That's all right,' she said, reaching for the doorhandle and wondering why he hadn't called her to cancel the evening.

'No, we're still going.'

Her hand stopped in mid-air and she turned to look at him.

'The Assistant Chief feels very bad about it so he said go anyway, at the expense of the force.'

She still didn't move or say anything.

'The Cloisters in Richmond. Very expensive, three Michelin-star food,' he coaxed.

Her hand fell back into her lap.

'Why not?'

'Why not, indeed,' he smiled and turned on the ignition.

CHAPTER TEN

'WELL, if it is not Daykin of Interpol,' said the custody sergeant cheerfully as Daykin walked into the charge office the following morning. He was holding out a piece of paper.

'Hilarious,' said Daykin, looking at the paper, 'what is it?'

'I don't know, it's in French.'

Daykin snatched it from the sergeant and read. It was from Sergent Dupont of the Paris police. He had made enquiries about Jonathan Lister. He stayed overnight at the Georges Cinq three or four times a year, arriving by taxi from the Porte de Vanves district where he always walked into the taxi office with his luggage. After one night in Paris he would catch the morning flight to Nice and six or seven days later would return to the Georges Cinq for one night. In the morning he would take a taxi back to the Porte de Vanves, get out of the cab and, effectively, disappear. He always paid his hotel bill and the taxi fares in cash. He is English, well-dressed and wealthy. And that is all anyone knew about him.

'Interesting, sir?' said Toby Peterson, looking over his shoulder.

'Only because it raises one question.'

'Which is?'

'Why does an old hotel bill paid by a man nobody knows anything about end up in a murdered man's jacket?'

'And the answer is?'

'I don't know. That's why I've got a job for you. Find out all you can about Jonathan Lister.'

'Starting with what?'

'With the fact that it's nearly impossible to lose yourself in this country. If you work, the Inland Revenue know where you are; if you don't the Benefit Agencies have you on file. Then there are credit card records, council taxes, hire-purchase agreements, passport applications, bank accounts, investments, property sales and purchases. You get the picture.'

The telephone on the custody desk rang. The sergeant picked it up, listened for ten seconds, then grunted into it before holding his hand over the receiver.

'Pathologist,' he said to Daykin, 'he's finished the post-mortem. Do you want to wait for the written report or get a verbal one from him now?'

'I'll see him now,' said Daykin. He looked at Toby Peterson, 'see what you can find by the time I get back.'

As Daykin got into his car Mark Jarvis was driving along the High Street towards the station.

Last night had been very satisfactory. He had not made any passes at Paula Sykes, that wasn't why he had invited her to dinner. All he wanted was to make her feel comfortable with him and to find out as much as possible about her.

So he had asked questions and listened attentively to her replies. She had told him a lot about herself, especially after the third glass of wine. She told him about her career in the army, though not about the affair or how she came to resign her commission. She had a deep and unexpected love of northern soul music and he listened to stories about Wigan Casino, James and Bobby Purefy, Eddie Floyd and a hundred other American singers whose records she had collected over the years. He nodded and smiled, but only to hide his indifference.

Eventually, she even told him about the scar on her face. She had been riding pillion on her boyfriend's motorcycle during the long summer vacation between her first and second years at university. They had been on their way down through France, heading for St Tropez. Somewhere between Orléans and Limoges they hit a piece of debris in the road and he, she and the motorcycle went three separate ways. Amazingly, her boyfriend got to his feet without a scratch, but the motorcycle, spinning gracefully as it slid across the road, collided violently with a wall and had to be written off.

In some ways she was lucky, she hardly touched the tarmac of the road before hitting the softer grass of a field and rolling over and over. Her luck ran out when her face hit the edge of a stone water trough, smashing the four upper left molar teeth, parts of which came out through her cheek. The surgeon was either incompetent, busy or drunk. He cut too deeply into the facial muscle, leaving her with the odd smile. It could, she said shrugging her shoulders as she must have done many times before, have been much worse.

Mark Jarvis spent most of the evening listening. He hinted that he and his wife lived separate lives. It wasn't true, but it would ease consciences when he and Paula Sykes eventually went to bed together.

He wasn't too pushy; you had to be so careful with people you worked with and he wasn't going to repeat the mistake he made last year. Misreading the signs from a female detention officer, he got a slap across the face. Then there were three months of uncertainty, she avoiding him and he wondering who she had told. Then he made the most of his luck. The custody sergeant told him that money had gone missing from prisoners' property. Only small amounts, but on a regular basis. He didn't know who was responsible, but she was the most likely candidate. Jarvis called her into his office and gave her an ultimatum, resign and get a month's pay or face disciplinary charges. She resigned and, as she was a civilian, he didn't even have to bother about the Police Federation.

When he dropped off Paula Sykes at her house she gave him a kiss on the cheek, just enough to show him that another invitation might well be accepted. Yes, it had all gone rather well. His reputation of a man who took advantage of a situation was well deserved.

It was a forty-mile drive to the Royal Hospital at Richmond, most of it on country roads, but the sun was shining, Daykin knew the roads well and there was little traffic, so he was there in well under an hour. He parked the car and walked through the impressive double door entrance. To his right, in a glass cubicle, sat an overweight receptionist, finishing the last of a packet of crisps.

'The mortuary?' asked Daykin politely.

She paid more attention to the inside of the crisp packet than she did to him.

'Basement. Turn right out of the lift.'

Daykin was not fond of lifts. This was one of those that are twice as long as they are wide, so they can fit trolleys in them and when the stainless steel doors shut he was in a metal cube with no contact with the outside world. This was the worst lift he had ever been in. With the squeak of unoiled bearings, the lift juddered to a halt and the doors slid slowly open.

The corridor that he stepped into was different to the ones above ground. The dull red linoleum floor and the battle-ship grey walls were the same, the lighting was dimmer, no one needed to see clearly here. And it was silent. The frantic shouting, the running, the harassed medics and worried relatives, the blood transfusions and saline drips were all in the past down here. There was no pain, no anxiety, no shock. That was for the living upstairs. Here there was only silence.

He had been to this urban mausoleum twice before and remembered where the post-mortem room was. He walked down the long corridor that smelt of disinfectant and formaldehyde. He knocked on the door at the far end.

It was opened by the small man with the broad smile.

'Inspector Daykin, dead on time.'

That was one of the ways Dr Caisley got through his day: he had a thousand jokes about death.

Caisley had always been small and even in his youth had been a bit overweight. But the years of eating his wife's cook-ing had left him with a stomach as large and round as a medi-cine ball, straining against a waistcoat that had been tailored for a much younger man. His hair, always unfashionably long, had now disappeared from his crown, leaving only a greying half circle at the back of his head, the hair falling over his collar in waves.

From a cheerful round face, his eyes twinkled behind a pair

of gold half-moon glasses. Daykin, who had known him for years, had always thought that if the local amateur dramatic society ever wanted to put on a production of *Pickwick* they had a lead who would only need the minimum of make-up.

'Come in, Inspector,' said Dr Caisley with a theatrical bow and a wave of his arms.

Daykin stepped from the dimness of the corridor into the bright post-mortem room, lit from overhead by rows of fluorescent lights and banks of spotlights. In the centre of the room was a single stainless-steel table which an assistant in green scrubs and wellington boots and a long maroon rubber apron was wiping down. He didn't look up as Daykin entered.

Doctor Caisley pulled the handle of a drawer in the bank on the far wall and the body of Michael Hilliam was rolled out. Caisley took the sheet away and, for the next fifteen minutes, described each of the wounds as he pointed to them with a small plastic ruler he took from his top pocket. The fatal blow had entered the chest at an angle of forty degrees and had been struck from behind by a man or woman who knew what they were doing, the blade had pierced the centre of the heart and death was instantaneous. The killer had almost certainly been trained in the services, probably special forces, possibly Royal Marine Commandos because that was how they are trained to kill with a knife. The blade would have been about eighteen centimetres long and double-edged.

'Double-edged, like a commando knife?'

'Possibly.'

'Why were the wounds made to the hands and feet?'

'That's a question for you; you're the detective. I'm just a simple pathologist.'

'Apart from the motive, that leaves another three questions.'

'Which are?'

'Why were those wounds made, why was Michael Hilliam in the church and who knew that he was there?'

'Well,' said Dr Caisley, closing the drawer, 'best of luck.'

Daykin looked at his watch as he left the hospital. It was late and he was tired, so he called the station and told them that he was going off duty. He drove home and cooked a goulash. He was a natural, self-taught cook. He could tell by reading a recipe what it would taste like and what could be added to improve it. His mother and sisters cooked well, but in the traditional farmhouse way, fresh ingredients, simply prepared. So did Jenny, but when he married her she learnt quickly from him. Each Saturday night when he was not on duty they would each cook one course of the evening meal. It was the only time there was any rivalry between them and they both tried their best to beat the other. He missed her every hour he was awake, but at times like these, cooking alone in the kitchen they had shared, he missed her most of all.

While the goulash simmered he took the dog for a short walk, then he ate the meal and went to bed early. He did not sleep well, the night was filled with images of hooded figures wielding knives and pale-skinned wide-eyed ghosts with wounds in their hands and feet.

That night The Feathers was busier than usual and, ignoring the licensing laws, closed nearly forty minutes after it should. An hour after the last loud customer had started to stagger home the staff, after cleaning up, filed out of the front door. Tony Hammond was the last to leave and as he locked the

73

door and walked away, shouting his goodnights to the others, the eyes that watched him carefully and coldly from the shadows of a doorway across the green were full of hate.

CHAPTER ELEVEN

WHEN Tom Daykin arrived at the station the following morning he found Toby Peterson standing in the car-park, watching a Portakabin that was to be their incident room being lowered by a crane from a lorry.

'What do you have for me?' asked Daykin.

'He doesn't exist.'

'Meaning?'

'There is no official record of him,' said Peterson. 'There are no tax records, no benefit claims; he doesn't own property or, for all that I can tell, even a car.'

'No finances?'

'No bank account, credit cards, loans or savings.'

'Passport?'

'There was one issued three years ago.'

'But?'

'All the details were false, the birth certificate was forged and the address it was sent to was demolished six months later.'

'Has the SOCO brought any documents from the victim's shop?'

'They're bagged up in the storeroom.'

'Let's go and get them. You're about to find out just how boring police work can be.'

Fifteen minutes later they stood in Daykin's office, surrounded by large clear plastic bags full of the trivia of Michael Hilliam's business life.

'There has to be another link between these two men and if it's there, it will be in the paperwork. Concentrate on that.'

For three long hours they waded through the bank statements, business invoices, correspondence and a thousand other pieces of paper of most colours and sizes. Finally, the bags resealed, they were left with three pieces of paper on Daykin's desk. Daykin had put them there; for all his hours of eyestraining work Toby Peterson had again found nothing. He turned the papers round to face him so he could read them. He didn't know what he had expected to see, but whatever it was, he was disappointed. Two petrol receipts and a paid invoice addressed to a man called Lister from a firm of estate agents. He looked up at Daykin.

'Why, out of all these mountains of paperwork, are these important, sir?'

'Start with the petrol receipts.'

Toby Peterson pulled up a chair to the desk and sat down on it. He looked at each of the receipts carefully. They were almost identical, issued by the same garage in Kent. They were computerized receipts, showing the time and date each was issued, how much fuel was purchased and from which pump. The first was issued at ten past eight on the evening of 14 March. It was dirt stained, as if it had been on the floor of a vehicle. Fifty-five litres of diesel had been bought from pump number 12. The other, crease marks running through it, showed forty-seven litres of diesel bought at five past seven the following morning from pump number 2.

Peterson reached for the other document, but Daykin stopped him.

'What do the receipts tell you?'

Toby Peterson placed the receipts carefully side by side on the desk top.

'Someone went to Kent in March and bought a lot of fuel.'

'Why?'

Toby Peterson stared hard at the receipts, hoping that he had missed something. He hadn't.

'Kent,' said Daykin. 'Dover, the Channel Tunnel, Seacat hovercraft, ferries. Four different ways to France.'

'And Michael Hilliam went to France to buy antiques,' said Peterson. He paused and looked again at the receipts. 'But if they're both his, he must have driven a long way through the night on the fourteenth to have to fill up again at seven the following morning.'

'There's another explanation,' said Daykin. 'Two different vehicles.'

'Why?'

Daykin pulled the other documents towards him.

'I'm hoping that this may tell us.'

Toby Peterson stood up and walked round the desk, so that he could look over Daykin's shoulder. He read the exhibit label attached to the invoice.

'Found at the back of a drawer,' he read out loud.

'So it could be that Mr Hilliam didn't know he had it,' said Daykin.

Peterson read the invoice, this time silently. It was from a firm of estate agents called Langley and Smart in Canterbury, addressed to Jonathan Lister. It was for six months' rent of a mews house in Ashford and someone had written on it in green ballpoint, 'Paid in cash'.

'There's a lot of cash floating around Mr Hilliam,' said Toby Peterson, 'and he seems to have a lot of Jonathan Lister's documents.'

'Yes,' said Daykin thoughtfully, 'that may be important.' He kept looking at the invoice for another minute then, pulling a plastic sleeve from his desk drawer, he slid all three documents into it.

'Ring the police station in Ashford and get hold of the duty inspector. We need a warrant to search that address.'

'Where are you going, sir?'

'To church; it's good for the soul.'

CHAPTER TWELVE

THE Reverend Robert Morton was a creature of habit. Monday was his day off. Tuesdays were for hospital visits and he always composed his sermon on Wednesday afternoons. His wife let Daykin into the rectory and showed him to the study.

'Sorry to interrupt you,' began Daykin.

'Not at all Inspector. To tell the truth, I could do with a break.'

Ever the optimist, he looked at Daykin and said, 'I don't suppose you know anything about Paul's Letters to the Romans?'

Daykin shook his head.

'No,' said Robert Morton absentedly, 'I didn't think so.'

He looked at the policeman, hoping for inspiration. He didn't find any.

'Still,' he said eventually, 'what can I do for you?'

'We didn't get the chance to talk properly the other day, now that the dust has settled a bit. I wonder if we could talk to you again about Mr Hilliam.'

Robert Morton was a gossip at heart, but spent most of his life keeping other people's secrets. The chance to tell tales was all too much for him and the words came flooding out.

'I have been thinking about it, Inspector,' he began slowly, but that was only to build up a head of steam. 'I know I said that he had no friends but there was – how can I put this? It's rather delicate.'

'A female friend?'

'There were a number of women in his life; he wasn't completely loyal to his wife I'm afraid, if what I have been told is true.'

'He didn't appear to be a ladies' man.'

'Oh believe me, Inspector, you never know. Michael had a certain charm and a twinkle in his eye. I didn't approve; I thought about asking him to step down as warden but how many of us can cast the first stone?'

'Any male friends?'

'Well,' said the vicar, back on the rails of gossip again, 'I don't know if you call him a friend, but he saw Tony Hammond, usually in the church and usually quite late.'

'How late?'

'Between nine and ten at night.'

'Do you know why they went to the church?'

'I never found the time to ask either of them; it didn't seem important.'

'How do you know that they met up?'

'Several people have either seen them going down the church path, or lights on in the church late at night. It must have been one or other of them, or both, as they were the only people who had keys, apart from Mrs Sheppard and she does not go out late at night.'

'Is that it for friends?' asked Daykin.

'As far as I know, yes.'

'Anything else you can tell us about him?'

Robert Morton hesitated.

'I don't like to speak ill of the dead.'

And Daykin was sure that he didn't.

'If it helps to capture his murderer, I'm sure you'll be forgiven,' he coaxed.

'Yes, quite. He was a gambler.'

'What sort of gambling'?'

'I only know about the horses. Last year The Feathers organized a small party to go to the Ybor meeting at York Races. Jim Barber was one of the party and as he went to place a bet, two positions along the counter was Michael Hilliam, putting on a lot of money. On the nose, I think it's called.'

'That doesn't make him a gambler.'

'No. He didn't see Jim, so, out of curiosity, Jim went back to the betting counter after each race and, sure enough, there was Michael Hilliam putting a lot of money on a horse.'

'Thank you, Vicar, I think I've disturbed your afternoon enough for now,' said Daykin, beginning to get out of the chair. But the Reverend Morton wasn't finished.

'And he was a bigot.'

'A what?'

'A bigot. Some of his views were too right wing for me. That was the other reason I thought seriously about asking him to step down from the post of warden, but he has been here for a long time and I'm the newcomer, so I'm afraid I didn't have the courage.'

'Thank you for your time, Vicar. It's been very informative.'

'Perhaps you will return the favour and come to church one Sunday, Inspector?'

Daykin didn't promise that he would, but it didn't seem a bad idea.

CHAPTER THIRTEEN

D^AYKIN decided not to go straight back to the station, he wanted to find out why Hammond and Hilliam were meeting so often late at night in the church.

There wasn't an early evening crowd at The Feathers, just a couple of shopkeepers, the local solicitor and a branch bank manager who stopped in for a couple of pints on their way home. By the time Daykin and Peterson arrived they had already drunk up and gone. Tony Hammond was in the cellar, changing the beer barrels. The barman called to him through the open hatchway. Hammond came up the wooden ladder. He was not in the best of tempers.

'I've told you everything I know,' he said, as he stepped on to the flooring behind the bar and closed the hatch cover, 'why don't you just let me get on with serving my customers?'

Daykin looked round the bar. It was empty. Tony Hammond needed reminding that this wasn't just a social call. He took his notebook out of his pocket and opened it on the bar top. He slowly and deliberately wrote the time in the margin, then looked up at Hammond.

'Why did you meet Michael Hilliam so often at the church late at night?'

'Who says I did?'

'A number of people.'

'Who?'

'People who can be trusted to tell the truth.'

'Are you saying I'm not?'

'I'm just asking a question.'

Tony Hammond took a half-pint glass and held it under the beer pump while he pulled the porcelain handle towards him, as if testing the pump pressure.

'When you went to the church, did you see the two wands in their stands either side of the nave?' he said, holding the glass up to the light to examine the clarity of the beer, then pouring it into the sink.

Daykin nodded.

'Those are the warden's wands, they are symbols of office. Mike and I had the responsibility for the upkeep of the church. If you want to talk about what needs repairing, what better place to meet?'

'Why late at night?'

'He didn't shut his shop until six o'clock. By the time he had driven home, had his tea and sorted himself out, at the earliest it would be half-past eight.'

'I can't see why you needed so many meetings: the church doesn't seem to be falling down to me.'

The anger returned to Tony Hammond's eyes.

'Do you think I killed him?'

Daykin said nothing.

'I only knew him through the church. What motive would I have to kill him?'

He had a point. Daykin put away his notebook.

'That's a good question,' he said. 'Thank you, Mr Hammond.'

'What are you saying?' said Tony Hammond, his voice coloured with more than a trace of mockery. 'Don't leave town?'

'If you did, we'd find you,' said Daykin.

Tony Hammond's smile broadened.

'Oh, I don't think you would,' he replied. There was something in the confident way he said it that made Tom Daykin think hard on the walk back to the car.

CHAPTER FOURTEEN

'THERE'S an Inspector Hyland in Ashford,' said Toby Peterson when Daykin got back to the station. 'Here's his phone number.'

Daykin phoned the inspector and asked him to get a warrant to search the house in Ashford, to send a team in to search it and to speak to the estate agents about the man who rented it.

'Thomas Daykin,' said the custody sergeant, pretending to search under the counter as Daykin walked past it on his way to the incident room.

'What are you looking for?' asked Daykin.

'Just seeing if I've got a spare set of full riot gear under here; you're going to need it. Chief Inspector Sykes wants to see you in her office and she's baying for blood.'

'She can bay all she wants. I'm going to get a large mug of coffee.'

Ten minutes later, with caffeine in his bloodstream and the dog settled in the corner of the incident room, he decided to face the music. He walked up the corridor and knocked on Paula Sykes's office door. He didn't have to wait long, she opened it herself.

'Come in, Inspector and sit down.'

If Paula Sykes was after Daykin's blood, she wasn't showing it.

As he sat down Daykin looked round the room. He realized that since she arrived six months ago, he had never been in this office. He had not even seen the inside of it, because on or off duty, present or absent, the door to Paula Sykes's office was always closed. She had not exactly stamped her personality on the room. Chief Inspector Ramsden had retired nearly nine months ago. This had been his office and apart from a small bunch of pansies in a cheap plastic vase on the windowsill, nothing had changed. The desk, chairs and cheap prints on the walls were all the same.

There was something, a picture of a young girl in a heart-shaped silver frame on the corner of the desk. Daykin had to lean slightly forward to see it properly. A pretty little girl. her blonde hair in bunches, tied with green velvet ribbons. She had a look of Paula Sykes, certainly a relative, perhaps a daughter or niece. Daykin's attention was suddenly refocused.

'I'm in charge of the administration at this station and although Superintendent Jarvis has overall responsibility for expenses, I need to know why they are incurred. Now, what's this about the cost of an incident room?'

Daykin wasn't sure what to say, but just then the cavalry arrived. There was a knock on the door and Sergeant Pullan opened it.

'Sorry to disturb you, ma'am, but there's a fax for Inspector Daykin, it looks urgent.'

Paula Sykes sighed. 'All right, Inspector Daykin, we'll finish this later.'

Daykin got up and followed the custody sergeant out of the office.

'Thanks, Harry.'

'You looked like you needed some help.'

As Daykin closed the office door Paula Sykes picked up the photograph of the child and gently stroked the frame for several seconds with a tenderness no one in the police station had ever seen, before replacing it on the desk.

'There, there, darling,' she said softly. 'Mummy will make it better.'

On his way to the charge office Daykin passed Superintendent Jarvis in the corridor. They did not speak, they both had other things on their minds.

Jarvis opened the door Daykin had just closed.

'Chief Inspector,' he began as Paula Sykes smiled that smile that he now found endearing, 'some administration problems have come up and I'd like to run them by you.'

She raised her eyebrows, but she was still smiling.

'They involve some of the staff,' he continued, 'and I don't want to be overheard. Any chance we could talk about them over a drink this evening?'

Paula Sykes wasn't going to make it easy for him; she knew this wasn't about staffing problems.

'I don't think I can make it this evening, sir.' The smile had now gone, replaced by a frown of regret.

'I would take it as a great personal favour,' persisted Jarvis.

'I suppose I could put off my plans for this evening,' she said doubtfully.

'I know a charming country pub, roaring fire and excellent bar snacks. I'll pay.'

The smile returned. 'How could I refuse?'

'Six-thirty, here?'

'Yes, sir.'

They had been on first name terms the other evening, but had agreed not to use them in the station. Besides, Jarvis liked it when she called him 'sir'.

CHAPTER FIFTEEN

INSPECTOR Hyland had worked fast and by ten the following morning was on the phone to Daykin.

He had been granted a warrant and they had searched the house in Ashford. They found a passport in the name of Jonathan Lister, a pair of expensive spectacles with plain glass in the frames, a bottle of hair dye and a wardrobe full of designer clothes. In the garage below the mews house was a white Mercedes Sprinter van.

The estate agents had rented the house over the phone and each six months they received the rent in cash in a recorded delivery envelope posted from an address in Boston, Lincolnshire. The same address, the DVLA said, as the van was registered. The inspector said that he had already posted the passport and would fax a copy of the DVLA document.

'What was all that about?" asked Toby Peterson, as Daykin switched off the speakerphone.

'It solves problems.'

'What problems?'

'Why Michael Hilliam's van was only doing about ten thousand miles a year and who Jonathan Lister is.'

'Who?'

'Michael Hilliam.'

Ten minutes later the fax arrived. Daykin read it.

'I'm going to Lincolnshire,' said Daykin, 'to see a woman called Pamela Horton, the owner of the van parked in the garage in Ashford. See what you can dig up on Tony Hammond while I'm away; I should be back early this evening.'

Parkland Avenue was a quiet middle-class street and Pamela Horton was a quiet middle-class woman. She was a small woman dressed entirely in beige and there was a resigned look on her face as if in the battle with life, she was losing heavily on points. She had the palest blue eyes he had ever seen, eyes that started watering with tears as soon as he produced his warrant card.

She had answered an advert in the local paper; she thought that it would be a job stuffing envelopes. Instead, the man on the phone told her he would pay her £120 a month to forward mail that arrived at her address to a PO box in Selby, to register a van in her name at her address and to register an envelope she would receive every six months and send it to some estate agents in Kent. He said that he was going through a messy divorce and the less his wife knew about his life the better. She didn't know if he was telling the truth, but the money, which arrived promptly in cash in a registered envelope on the first of each month, came in very handy.

'The mail you sent to Selby, who was it addressed to?'

'Mr J. Lister.'

She had never met the man and had only spoken to him on the phone twice.

Daykin left her, a tiny beige tearful bag of nerves. Before he left he told her that no one was going to take her to court, but she didn't believe him.

Leaving Boston, he drove across country, almost due west, to the A1 and then headed north on the A63 directly into the small market town of Selby.

At the post office he met Mrs Smallwood, a small dumpy woman with loosely fitting clothes and tightly permed hair, who was in charge of the PO boxes.

For fifteen minutes they talked about Box 305. It had been hired by Mr Lister about six months ago. He had telephoned to arrange to hire it and a few days later had sent the money for three months rental in cash, with a short note. She showed him the note, it was written on a computer on plain paper and was simply signed 'L'. Not even enough for a handwriting expert to work on. He paid in cash in advance every three months and, although he must empty the box occasionally, so far as she was aware no one had seen him.

CHAPTER SIXTEEN

IT was late afternoon when Daykin cupped his hands round the steaming mug of tea he had just made and went to find Toby Peterson.

'Seen Toby Peterson, Harry?' he asked the custody sergeant.

'Try your state-of-the-art incident room,' said the sergeant, without looking up from the early edition of the evening paper.

Daykin walked across the car-park to the newly installed Portakabin and opened the door. He was surprised by what he saw. A blackboard running the breadth of the far wall had been screwed into position. Several tables lined two walls and on them were half-a-dozen telephones. In the far corner was a fax machine and a photocopier.

But he knew that they were really in business when he saw, in the other corner, a water cooler and a coffee machine.

With his back to him, writing all they knew about Michael Hilliam's death on the blackboard, was Toby Peterson.

'Why six telephones?' asked Daykin.

Peterson, who had not heard him come in, spun round in surprise.

'Superintendent Jarvis has assigned us two CIDs and three uniforms, starting tomorrow at nine in the morning, sir.'

'Then,' said Daykin, pulling the top two stacking chairs from a pile, 'you'd better know as much as I do.'

Toby Peterson took out his notebook and settled himself into a chair.

'Write in that, "Briefed by Inspector Daykin", then put it away. You don't want some smart arse barrister making you look stupid by examining your notebook.'

Sergeant Peterson did as he was told. When the notebook was back in his pocket, Daykin said, 'What do you know about Michael Hilliam?'

'Antique dealer. Mid-forties. Divorced. Had lived locally for years, for the last few years alone and with no current girl-friend, unless you count the ones the vicar spoke about. A shop in Asquith. Bought a lot of his antiques from France and he was Jonathan Lister.' He paused. 'You didn't tell me why you thought that they were both the same man.'

'Who is the only person who can describe Jonathan Lister?'

'Yvette Benastre.'

'And she did not see him very often. What are the differences in the descriptions of the two men?'

'Lister had dark hair, wore glasses and was ten years younger.'

'So probably the same height and build. Different clothes, but that doesn't mean different people. The glasses were fitted with plain glass, so the wearer didn't need them, except as a disguise.'

'Now,' he said, getting up, 'it's been a long day, I'm going home. Nine o'clock, here?'

Toby Peterson got up and started to stack his chair back on to the pile.

'Oh,' said Daykin, 'I almost forgot. What did you find out about Tony Hammond?'

Peterson stopped, put the chair down and took out his notebook again, while he flipped through the pages to the day's entries.

'You're not going to like it.'

'Try me.'

'He's another mystery man.'

'Meaning?'

'He came to this village about two years ago. Before that, there's nothing about him, anywhere.'

'Where have you tried?'

Toby Peterson started reading from his notebook.

'His driving licence was issued two years ago. There is no trace of any previous licence, or of him ever passing a driving test. His passport was issued at about the same time. No previous passports and nothing at the Passport Office in London showing an application form. When he arrived here he opened a bank account in Camleigh. There is no evidence of any other bank account with his bank, or any other bank. By coincidence. I have a schoolfriend who is now pretty high up at that bank and I called in a favour. He shouldn't tell me, but he says that on the first working day of each month a sum of money is paid into that account by telegraphic transfer. When he tried to trace the source of the money, all he got was "access denied". He doesn't have any credit cards now and there is no trace of him ever having had one. I've searched against property, income tax, criminal record, marriage, children and state benefits. All negative, both now and at any time.'

'So we know that he exists now, but over two years ago, he didn't?'

'That's about the size of it, sir.'

'As I said, it's been a long day. Do you fancy a beer?'

'That's the best offer I've had today.'

'Follow me.'

When Toby Peterson first met Daykin he had seen an over-weight, middle-aged man in creased corduroy trousers and one of the collars of his shirt, trapped by the lapel of his shabby tweed sports jacket, sticking up at an odd angle towards his chin. He thought that Daykin's cottage would be the same shambles as the man. As he walked through the front door he saw that he was wrong. Both inside and outside the building it was well maintained. The carpets were recently vacuumed, the furniture though old was well cared for and, from what he could see of the kitchen, everything was in place, clean and tidy.

Daykin showed him into the living-room and then walked off down the hallway. Toby Peterson was left in a small rectangular room, the far wall dominated by a floor-to-ceiling bookcase which was full to overflowing with rows of hard-back books. Peterson had lent his head to one side as he began to look through the titles when Daykin reappeared with an open bottle of beer and a tall glass.

'Hungry?' he said, handing the bottle and glass to Toby Peterson.

'Famished.'

Daykin nodded and left the room again. Peterson poured some of the beer, and tilted the bottle so he could read the label. It was a Czech lager he had never heard of. He took a swig from the glass then, bored with his own company, walked towards the kitchen.

Tom Daykin was chopping onions. He bent low over the board like a professional chef, the blade of the large knife carving through the onion in rapid slices. On the hob was a copper frying pan, the butter in it starting to sizzle as it melted into a small pool of oil. Daykin picked up the chopping board and, with the back of the knife blade, scraped the onions into the pan. He tossed the onions several times to coat them with the butter and oil mixture then took a clove of garlic from a terracotta pot by the bread crock. He peeled the garlic, pushed it into a garlic press and squeezed it over the onions.

It was a tiny kitchen and the fridge was only two paces behind Daykin. He turned, opened the door and took out a bunch of parsely and two chicken breasts on a small plate. He tossed the pan again, and put the chicken breasts into it. Then he began to chop the parsley.

'In a blue and white jug in the fridge you'll find some chicken stock. Make yourself useful and pour five ounces into the measure, will you?' said Daykin over his shoulder, nodding at the measuring jug in front of him.

While Toby Peterson poured the stock Daykin slid the chopped parsley into the pan and turned the chicken over. Then he poured the stock over it and, taking a bottle of wine from the fridge, uncorked it and poured about a quarter of the bottle into the pan.

'That'll be about twenty minutes,' he said. 'Are you OK with beer, or do you want some wine?'

'The beer's good.'

Daykin opened a cupboard door and took out a wine glass. He poured some of the wine from the opened bottle into it.

'Well, Toby, what do you do to relax?'

'Nothing much,' mumbled Toby Peterson.

There was reluctance in his voice and Daykin was too good a policeman to miss it.

'Come on,' he coaxed, 'everyone has a hobby.'

He looked at Peterson. but said nothing else. Countless interviews had taught him that sometimes silence was the best question.

'Military miniatures,' said Peterson eventually.

'Toy soldiers?'

'They are not toy soldiers, they are die-cast metal minatures, correct in every detail.'

'And you do what with them? Fight battles?'

'No, that's war-gaming.' Toby Peterson paused. 'I do that too.'

'You mean this time Napoleon wins at Waterloo?'

'He nearly did. He was heavily outnumbered and sent part of his army to hold up von Blücher's arrival so he could take the battle to the British on their own. Then, with the first charge, he split Wellington's army in two. For hours it could have gone either way. Finally Napoleon sent in his cavalry to crush the British infantry in what he thought was the winning throw of the dice.'

'What happened?'

'The British infantry square. It was one of those military inventions that turns history. Up to then it was a rule of battle that infantry couldn't stand up to a cavalry charge, but the square had three ranks of troops on each side and those troops could fire their muskets every fifteen seconds, so as the French cavalry came up the hill they were hit by a volley of bullets every five seconds.'

'End of battle?'

'Not quite, Napoleon still had a trick or two up his sleeve, but then von Blücher arrived and it was game over.'

'So Napoleon didn't get the praise he deserved.'

'The victor always rewrites history.'

97

Daykin drained the last of the wine from his glass.

'The cutlery is in the top drawer and the place mats are on top of the wine rack; set the table, will you?' he said, as he opened the door to the larder and picked out a packet of pasta. While the pasta cooked he finished off the sauce, adding cream and a teaspoon of mustard. Ten minutes later they were sitting at the kitchen table.

Toby Peterson didn't know what to call Daykin off duty, so he didn't call him anything.

'And you,' he said, as he finished the first mouthful of chicken, 'do you have any hobbies?'

'Cooking, and I read a bit.' Daykin stopped, it sounded like something a Miss World contestant would say.

'Rugby, I watch rugby. And I train the district police team. Do you play?'

'I played at school. Badly.'

'Pity.'

'They say,' said Toby Peterson, 'that you were in line for an England cap.'

'They exaggerate.'

'It's what I've been told. You played for Yorkshire, the next step is international.'

Daykin poured himself some more wine.

'Maybe. If my luck hadn't run out. But there's no use dwelling on maybes, you can't change the past.'

'I'm sorry about your wife.'

'Thanks.'

Toby Peterson thought that that was all he was going to say.

'She was beautiful,' said Daykin, talking more to himself than Toby, 'far too good-looking for the likes of me. She was everything I'm not. Popular, sophisticated, well dressed though, to be honest, she would have looked good in a bin liner. She had glorious chestnut-coloured hair. Warm hearted and always laughing. Do you know what I first liked about her?'

He didn't wait for an answer.

'Her voice. I can close my eyes and hear it now. Soft, too soft to be husky, but sort of deep and breathy at the same time. A voice you don't hear twice in your life.'

He took another drink of wine, more a gulp than a sip this time.

'The only cruel thing she ever did in her life was to leave me with so many memories and so much unsaid and undone.'

It was after midnight when Toby Peterson left the house. He left with the feeling that he knew Daykin a bit better, but that there was still a lot left to know.

At almost the same time Mark Jarvis was opening Paula Sykes's garden gate on his way to the car. It had been another good evening, but one of mixed messages. As they got off their bar stools her hand had brushed against his knee and he tried to persuade himself that it had been deliberate. When he stopped the car outside her house and as she unbuckled her seatbelt he said hopefully, 'Coffee?'

She gave him a stern look.

'All right, but just coffee, Mark, understood?'

They only had coffee and talked, but as he left the house an hour later she again gave him a kiss on the cheek, this time her lips resting a fraction longer on his skin, letting him smell her perfume and feel her warm breath.

It was enough to make him think of her all the way home.

CHAPTER SEVENTEEN

IT was a slow, steady rhythm, relentlessly pounding double beats somewhere between his temples. Daykin woke slowly and it took him some time to understand that he was listening to the sound of his own heartbeat. He opened his eyes, far too quickly and the heartbeat became the soundtrack to a blurred kaleidoscope of colours. He groaned loudly then wished he hadn't as the sound of his voice rattled painfully round the inside of his skull.

As gently as he could he sat upright in bed and tried to force his vision into focus. And then he remembered.

Since his wife's death there were evenings that were better than others, evenings when he cooked or read or watched some television. Then there were the evenings when the black depression settled on him, gripping him in a melancholic embrace. On those evenings he either sat and wallowed in self-pity or he took to the bottle. Last night had been a bottle night. He remembered opening one bottle of claret after Toby left. Had there been a second? He decided not to think about it and, putting on his glasses. turned back to focusing on the room. When the picture cleared it told its own story. The clothes that he had been wearing last night were scattered across the floor, the chair lay on its side by the door. He must have tried and failed to get into his pyjama trousers which now lay in a tangled heap by the bed. He had managed the jacket, but only one of the buttons was fastened. He groaned again, got out of bed and stumbled towards the shower.

The weather had changed overnight. Grey overcast skies had given way to sunshine through high cirrus clouds and, driving in to the station, the hangover rinsed away by the shower, Daykin found himself humming softly.

Although he was expecting it, it still came as a surprise to him to see people working in the incident room. One of the bonuses of a small station was that he knew them all, even the ridiculously young woman police constable who would, unfortunately, get the jobs no one else wanted to do. He might try to stop that but knew he wouldn't be successful. Toby Peterson had staked his claim to his desk at the end of one of the tables. He had spread out a pencil box, his car keys and his notebook to mark out the territory. Daykin pulled out a chair and slid it beside him.

He looked round the room at the faces staring back at him.

'For those of you who don't know him, this is Detective Sergeant Peterson. If you have anything to report and I'm not here you can tell him, he has my complete trust.'

Toby Peterson took his turn to look at the faces now looking at him. If any of them were surprised that he had Daykin's complete trust, they weren't any more amazed than he was.

'Let me make the introductions,' said Daykin, as he got up, walked behind the nearest chair and put both hands on the shoulders of the uniformed constable sitting in front of him.

'Jason Pullan,' he said. 'Jason's been with us for about four years.' Jason nodded. 'And if you notice any resemblance to

Harry Pullan, our custody sergeant, it's because Jason is his son.'

Daykin took a short step sideways and put one hand on the shoulder of the other male uniformed officer. 'This is Trevor Crossley. Trevor went through school, police training and their first four years in the force with Jason, but next month there is a parting of the ways. Trevor is going off on an advanced driving course and then to the road traffic motorway patrol.'

'When God decided to give a gift to women,' continued Daykin, walking to stand behind the first of the CID officers, 'He made Terry Harvey.'

Harvey smiled at everyone in the room to show that he agreed, the smile broadening by a fraction when his gaze fell on Constable McKenzie. Harvey was wearing a T-shirt and casual trousers, both with discreet designer labels and Toby Peterson knew enough about shoes to recognize expensive and Italian. 'Don't let him near your girlfriend,' said Daykin.

'Martin Reynolds,' said Daykin, now standing behind the other CID officer. He was also casually dressed, but the T-shirt was from a supermarket shelf, the trousers were baggy and creased and the trainers scuffed and dirty.

'Martin may look like a bag lady, but he knows everything that goes on in this town and for ten miles around, so if you want any local knowledge, ask him.'

'And finally, Gillian McKenzie.' All eyes turned to the young woman, whose face coloured and she looked down at her shoes. 'Gillian hasn't been here long, but she has all the qualities to make a first-class officer.'

Daykin may have been kind, but although the girl's face coloured a bit more, his words gave her the courage to look up and face the men in the group.

Daykin went back to sit beside Toby Peterson.

'We are waiting for the pathologist's report, but that won't tell us anything new. I need the summaries of the fingertips searches and the house-to-house enquiries. Put the DCs on the job of going into the lives of Michael Hilliam and Tony Hammond. Tell them I don't want to see them until they have something to report. Prepare a correlation sheet of all the intelligence in this case. If you can't beg, steal or borrow a computer use that laptop of yours and bill the force. Get on to the Kent Police, tell them to send a SOCO team to the house in Ashford. I want tapings off every fabric surface. Empty the wardrobes and examine all the clothing for documents, hair, skin flakes, anything to get a DNA match. I want the finger-print people and the stolen vehicles squad to go over the van with a fine-tooth comb. Find out where it was bought, who bought it and where it has been since then. Get the uniforms to take detailed statements from the vicar, Miss Murgatroyd, Mrs Hilliam and anyone else you can think of. Is that enough for now?'

Toby Peterson, who had been scribbling furiously, nodded.

'Where can I contact you, sir?'

'I'm going over to the shop in Asquith. We've missed something there and I want to take another look at it.'

Before he left, Daykin telephoned the estate agents. They told him that Mrs Potterton had agreed with Michael Hilliam's estate that she would run the shop and sell off the stock.

Daykin drove to Asquith, parked his car and, on the promise of a walk later on, told the dog to wait. He strolled to the shop. Mrs Potterton was standing in the window, taping up Sale signs. A man's death has many effects.

He showed her his warrant card and introduced himself.

'I'm Tom Daykin and I'm looking into Mr Hilliam's death. I wonder if I can take a look round the shop?'

Mrs Potterton seemed distracted and told him to do whatever he needed to, then she went back to her window and the signs. There was a faint redness round the eyes, as if she had been crying. Daykin wondered if there was more to her relationship with Michael Hilliam than shopkeeper and part-time assistant. Perhaps the vicar was right about his effect on women.

Daykin walked straight to the office and opened the desk. He took out the small black lever arch file of bank statements, a box of receipts and the handwritten ledgers. He stacked them neatly on the floor. He spent the next ninety minutes making a thorough search of the desk, but found nothing to interest him. He picked up the pile of documents from the floor and carried it into the shop showroom.

'I'm taking these for a few days, if you don't mind.' Mrs Potterton shook her head, looking through the window at something in the distance, not at him.

He asked her about the stock in the shop. She told him that about half of it was French and although the English antiques sold better and he usually sold the French ones through the trade at about what he paid for them, perhaps he just enjoyed the trips to France. Michael Hilliam paid her eighty pounds a day while he was away, double what the Trustees now paid.

An electronic buzzer sounded as the door to the shop opened and two customers walked in. Daykin was finished anyway.

'Thank you for your time, Mrs Potterton. I'll bring these documents back in a few days.'

He did not carry the documents far. He walked down the High Street until he reached a hardware shop. He opened the front door and walked in. It was the type of shop that, except in small country villages like this, the multi-national super-stores had put out of business years ago. It was a shop wider than it was long, but it appeared narrow as the walls were hung with every type of tool and, in front of them, racks of plastic packets containing screws, nuts, bolts and hooks, arranged in sizes and colours. As the window was covered with a display of household goods which blotted out all the daylight in the interior of the shop, the only light came from four electric lightbulbs each covered by a dark-green metal shade. The shop itself smelt of forgotten odours, beeswax, linseed oil and paraffin. At the far end, behind a wooden counter which had the dark lustre of decades of daily polishing, stood an old man in a brown overall. He wore a shirt and tie, a moustache which matched his steel grey centre-parted hair and heavy black-framed glasses. He looked as if he had been standing in this same spot five days a week since he was a young man. He had.

'Andy in, Mr Liddle?' asked Daykin.

'No, Tom, he's taking the day off.'

Tom Daykin had known Andy Liddle since they were at grammar school together. After qualifying as a chartered accountant he had set up an office above his father's shop and prepared the accounts for most of the local businesses. He wasn't ever going to die of overwork. He worked from nine until one, then walked the 200 yards to have lunch with his wife at home, returning at 2.30 and leaving as the village clock struck 5. He didn't work weekends. Ever.

'Can I leave these accounts and ask him to call me later today?'

'Day off, Tom.'

'It's important.'

'I'll try.'

The drive back to the station was delayed by a flock of sheep being moved across the narrow lane but Daykin didn't mind, he was used to it, and, anyway, it gave him time to think.

When he got back to Shapford, Toby Peterson was alone in the incident room.

'Where is everybody?' asked Daykin.

'Uniforms are out taking statements, CID said you said not to come back until they have something to report.'

'See if you can get them all back here in half an hour, will you?'

Daykin started to walk to the door.

'Where shall I say you are, sir?'

'Taking the dog for a walk.'

The hills above the town had always been his favourite place. He used to come up here for walks with Jenny. As the dog bounced around chasing imaginary rabbits, he watched the wind trace its sweeping pattern through the long grass and listened to it rattle the leaves on the trees. He thought about the death of Michael Hilliam, Jonathan Lister and how he funded his lifestyle. He thought about the lack of motive and suspects. And he thought that his detective sergeant was coming along nicely and could well make a very good copper.

When he had had enough, he whistled for the dog and the pair of them walked back to the station and into the incident room. The dog, at first curious about this new room, quickly found itself a corner and settled down. Toby Peterson looked at it suspiciously before Daykin caught his attention.

'Can everyone sit down please. Sergeant?'

Peterson and the five other officers sat at a table.

For the next thirty minutes he went round the table, asking

each of them what they had. The pathologist said death was between 9 p.m. and 11 p.m., the crime scene investigator said that death occurred where the body was found, the search of the church and house-to-house were negative. After they had finished and Terry Harvey told him that Inspector Hyland could get a warrant the following morning, he told them all to ask questions about Tony Hammond.

'You fancy him for this, don't you, sir?' asked Jason Pullan.

'I think he has something to do with it, yes.'

CHAPTER EIGHTEEN

WORD about Tony Hammond didn't take long. Two hours after the incident room discussion, Martin Reynolds knocked on Daykin's office door.

'Can you spare half an hour, sir?'

Daykin put the intelligence reports to one side.

'What have you got?'

'I've got Red Malcolm in reception.'

'Malcolm Proctor?'

'In his anorak.'

Malcolm Proctor was known to everyone as Red Malcolm because winter or summer, snow, rain or shine he wore the same red anorak.

'What does he want?'

'Says he has some information on Tony Hammond.'

'You'd better show him in.'

There it was as he came through the office door, the red anorak. Daykin pretended to cough to hide a smile.

'Inspector Daykin,' said Malcolm Proctor, holding out his hand and beaming at Daykin as if they were old friends.

'Please sit down, Mr Proctor. Coffee?'

'White, three sugars,' said Proctor over his shoulder to Reynolds.

Reynolds went out of the room to make some coffee and Daykin took a closer look at Malcolm Proctor, a man he had only ever seen before at a distance. He was a small man, no more than 5'4", probably in his early forties but with one of those sad-eyed, lined faces that made judging his age very difficult. Under the anorak he wore a cardigan and a poloneck sweater, although the day was warmer than usual. In his hand he held his other identity badge, a dark-blue Greek fisherman's cap that he always wore outdoors.

Daykin took off his glasses, breathed on the lenses and polished them with the end of his tie. Taking the hint, Malcolm Proctor took off his own glasses, held them up to the light and looked hard at the lenses, the ageless lined face distorting as he narrowed his eyes against the light. Satisfied that the glasses did not need cleaning, he put them back on as the coffee arrived.

'Will there be anything else, sir?' asked Reynolds, as he bowed ironically to Malcolm Proctor.

'No, thank you,' said Proctor, the irony lost on him.

Daykin nodded to Martin Reynolds to sit in the chair beside Proctor and take notes.

'Well, Mr Proctor,' he said, 'what can you tell us about Tony Hammond?'

This was Malcolm Proctor's big moment; he did not get many and he was determined to make the most of it. He put his mug of coffee carefully on the beer mat Daykin used as a coaster, selected a biscuit from the small plate Martin Reynolds had brought in, took a bite and slowly chewed and swallowed before he spoke.

'As you know,' he began eventually, 'I live just across the

road from Mr Hammond and whilst I don't pry, you under-stand, I do see a lot of his comings and goings.'

'And?' prompted Daykin, feeling the first stabs of impa-tience.

'He went away overnight occasionally.'

'Why should that interest us?'

'Because several times, late at night, I saw that dark-blue van of poor Mr Hilliam call at his house, Tony Hammond got in and they drove off together.'

'How long was he away?'

'Just overnight. Except the last time.'

'Tell me about the last time.'

Malcolm ran a finger down the side of his nose. It was a strange, nervous gesture. It was time to tell his big secret.

'It was about three weeks ago,' he began, 'I'd been talking to Michael Hilliam the day before in the greengrocers, it must have been his half-day at the shop.' Daykin nodded furiously. It didn't make Malcolm Proctor get to the point any faster.

'He said that he was taking one of his trips to France and I made a joke of it, I said did he want anyone to carry his bags? He made a point, a bit too forcefully if you ask me, that he always went alone, so he didn't have to worry about what anyone else was doing.'

He reached for another biscuit, but Daykin put a hand on his wrist to stop him.

'What happened then?' he asked.

'Well,' said Malcolm Proctor, pulling his empty hand back, 'you can imagine my surprise when early the following morning I'm taking the milk in and I see Michael Hilliam's Transit van pull up outside Tony Hammond's house, Hammond comes running out, gets in and they drive off. That time he was away for nearly a week.'

'How do you know?'

'Because I saw Hilliam drop him back outside his house late at night.'

'How long before he was murdered?'

'About ten days.'

'Anything else you can tell us?'

'About Tony Hammond?'

'Yes.'

Malcolm Proctor thought for several seconds.

'Only this: in the few days before he moved into the house there were three or four odd-looking men there. They were dressed like workmen, but if you watched them carefully you could see that they weren't.'

'Who do you think they were?'

'I'm sure I don't know; all I know is that they weren't work-men.' He patted his pocket. 'Do you mind if I smoke?' Daykin shook his head.

'Thank you for your time, Mr Proctor, if you go with Constable Reynolds he'll take a full statement from you.' He offered Malcolm Proctor another biscuit as a consolation prize.

When they had gone, Daykin leaned back in his chair and polished his glasses again. He thought for a long time about what had just been said by Proctor. Then he finished his coffee and walked to the incident room.

Toby Peterson was just putting the telephone down as he came into the room.

'Bad timing, sir.'

Daykin looked at him quizzically.

'That was Inspector Hyland; he wanted a chat with you, but he's had to go out now. He said he'd call back later. I told him you were interviewing a witness.'

'I was. And what he told me made me think. See if you agree with this. Michael Hilliam lived a pretty normal life, except for the flat in Ashford and his trips to France. Now I hear that Tony Hammond may know more about the flat and the trips than he's told us so far. The relationship between Michael Hilliam and Tony Hammond is starting to look interesting.'

'And now there is only one person alive who can tell us about that.'

'Exactly. Let's take a drive to have another chat with Mr Hammond.'

It was too early for Tony Hammond to be at The Feathers, so they drove to his home. He answered the door in a pair of jeans and a vest. Although it was late he had stubble on his face and he looked as if he had not been up for long. Over the vest a small gold coin hung from his neck on a gold chain. Daykin noticed that on his forearm was an area of scarring, as if a tattoo had been surgically removed.

'What now?' demanded Hammond. He was not as co-operative as the last time they saw him.

'Can we have a chat?' asked Daykin.

'About what?' asked Hammond, standing squarely in the doorway and showing no sign of letting them in.

'Your trips with Michael Hilliam.'

It was only momentary, but there was a look of doubt or panic on Tony Hammond's face. But when he spoke again, he was calm and in control.

'Why don't you come in?' he said, stepping back into the hall to let them into the house.

When Daykin thought about it later, the short walk from the doorstep to the living-room gave Tony Hammond just enough time to think.

'What do you mean, "trips with Michael Hilliam"?' asked Hammond as they sat down in the living-room.

'We understand that you made several overnight trips with him and recently a trip to France lasting several days.'

'Who told you that?' asked Hammond, searching to see if they had good information, or if they were just fishing.

'It's reliable.'

'Who?' repeated Hammond.

Daykin thought that he knew Tony Hammond. He had seen hundreds of Tony Hammonds over the years. Manipulative, calculating and dishonest. He saw all their faces in Hammond's face now as it stared back at him impassively, ready to lie so convincingly.

'Michael Hilliam's dark-blue Transit van ring any bells with you? Calling to pick you up here late at night or early in the morning? You've been seen. Why take those trips with Hilliam and not tell us. Something to hide?'

'He gave me a lift a couple of times to see some friends, that's all. And I've never been to France in my life.'

'Why don't you cut the crap and tell the truth just once in your life. If you made that trip to France in Michael Hilliam's van we'll be able to prove it, there are cameras everywhere.'

Daykin looked carefully into the face. Was that a trace of a smile?

'Don't waste your time, Inspector. I've never been to France with Michael Hilliam or anyone else and you can look at all the closed circuit television footage you want, I won't be on it.'

He seemed very confident and Daykin guessed that he wasn't bluffing. He switched subjects.

'Where did you live before you came to Camleigh?'

The question threw him. The hint of a smile vanished instantly.

'What has that got to do with anything?' he said cautiously.

'It's a simple question,' replied Daykin.

'My private life has nothing to do with Mike's murder.'

That was the second time Daykin had heard Hammond call Michael Hilliam 'Mike', no one else had. Perhaps Malcolm Proctor was right, they were more than just churchwardens in the same church.

'I believe it may have.'

'Look, Inspector, I'm not a suspect, I'm not under arrest and I'm not going to answer any more questions. You'd better leave.'

He was rattled. Hammond had the right to tell him to leave, but Daykin wasn't ready to go just yet.

'Forget the trip to France, tell me about the overnight trips.'

But Hammond had had enough. Either the question about his former life had got to him or he was fed up with the questions. He got out of his seat.

'I'd like you to leave. Now.'

Daykin knew that the conversation was over, but he had one last try.

'If you don't speak to us now, you might have to later, somewhere less comfortable.'

'I said get out,' said Hammond, his voice rising towards a shout. He walked towards the door to open it for them as a final physical sign that they were not wanted in his home. Then he stopped, the door half open, as if he had just thought of something.

'Your source,' he said sarcastically, 'it's that prat Proctor isn't? Red bloody Malcolm with nothing to do except peep from behind his curtains and tell tales. Before you take his word as gospel, just think about this, he isn't lily white.'

'Isn't he?' asked Daykin, not moving from the sofa. This

was getting more interesting by the minute.

'When he next comes crawling to you with more village gossip, ask him why that tart from your station has been visiting him.'

'WPC McKenzie has been asked to make house-to-house enquiries,' said Peterson from the chair in the corner. He thought that he had better say something.

'Not her, the one with pips on her shoulders!'

'Chief Inspector Sykes?' asked Daykin.

'That's her! Ask him what he's been saying to her. Now leave.'

Daykin got up, he wouldn't get any more out of Tony Hammond today, but there would be other days. He and Toby Peterson walked out of the house, down the path and got into the car.

'What do you make of that?' asked Daykin as he put the key into the ignition.

'Depends what you mean, sir. His trips to France, his overnight trips, his former life, or Chief Inspector Sykes?'

Daykin didn't start the engine. Instead, he took off his glasses and absently swung them gently in circles by one of the arms.

'The trip to France. He seemed very sure that we wouldn't see him on any camera.'

'Which means he hasn't been to France.'

'Or that we wouldn't recognize him.'

'What about the overnight trips?'

'We know which vehicle he went in, so talk to Traffic about tapes from any surveillance cameras in the area and check the speed cameras, if any of them have film in them. And I think we had better get an expert to look at the van.'

'Expert?'

'He's retired now, which means he has all the time in the world, but I used to work with a Scenes of Crime Officer called Ted Kenningham. Best I ever saw, I'll give him a call and see if he'll do me a favour.'

They sat in silence for a few minutes.

'What do you think set him off like that when you asked him where he used to live?' asked Toby Peterson eventually.

'I don't know,' said Daykin, who had finished playing with his glasses and put them back on, 'but it's something to do with you not finding anything about his past. I'm not sure it's directly connected to the murder, but it might help us find out.'

'And Chief Inspector Sykes?'

'Now there is a mystery. Hopefully, the easiest one to solve, we'll just ask her.'

'We?'

Daykin smiled.

'You're right. I'd better do that on my own. You never know what answer she'll give.'

CHAPTER NINETEEN

Dᴀʏᴋɪɴ had decided to leave the interview with Chief Inspector Sykes until the following morning when, refreshed by breakfast, the thoughts of a new day and with caffeine flowing through her veins, she might be in a good mood. He stood in front of her door, closed as usual, and knocked.

'Come in,' she called. It was difficult to tell in just two words, but she seemed in a good mood. Daykin opened the door and put his head round it.

'Do you have five minutes, ma'am?'

She looked at him with a steady, unblinking gaze. Perhaps he had been wrong about her mood. She straightened the papers on the desk in front of her with exaggerated care, to show that she was not pleased at being interrupted.

'Sit down, Inspector. As long as it is only five minutes.'

Daykin sat down. He was going to pull out his notebook, but thought better of it. 'I'm told,' he began softly, 'that you have been to see Malcolm Proctor at his home.'

'Who told you that?'

Could no one answer a straight question? This time there was nothing to be gained by hiding the informant.

117

'Anthony Hammond.'

Paula Sykes picked up a paper knife and examined it, revolving it between the fingers of both hands.

'This has nothing to do with your case, or I would have mentioned it to you. Yes, I visited that piece of shit Proctor once at his home.'

Daykin had never heard her swear before and both the word and the venom surprised him.

'Why did you go to his house?'

'When I came here,' she began, talking mainly to the paper knife, 'I was asked to be liaison with Child Protection. About a month ago we got a fax from the FBI in Washington to say that they had been investigating a child pornography site in America and Malcolm Proctor's details had come up as accessing the site on a number of occasions.'

'So you went to see him?' asked Daykin, surprised. They both knew the procedure, she should have reported it to the Child Protection Team and let them deal with it.

'I wanted him to know what was coming to him,' she said. 'I wanted him to know that someone in this area knew what a perverted little pillock he is. I wanted him to suffer just that bit more.'

There was a bitterness in her voice, something had generated emotions Daykin hadn't seen before. Then he saw again the photograph of the child on her desk. She said nothing for thirty seconds, as if the conversation they had just had was over.

'Is that your daughter?' he asked leaning to pick up the picture frame.

With a speed that caught him off guard, she snatched the picture from the desk, as if protecting the child.

'She was,' she said, the colour rising in her face. 'She was killed in a car crash about two years ago.'

'I'm sorry,' he said. He couldn't think of anything else to say.

'Well, if that's all, Inspector,' said Paula Sykes, placing the photograph back on the desk and picking up some papers.

'I take it you did report the matter to the Child Protection Team, ma'am?'

'Of course I did!'

Paula Sykes started writing notes on the papers on her desk. She didn't look up.

'You've had your five minutes, Inspector.'

Daykin got up and left the office. He walked through the charge office, across the car-park and into the incident room. Toby Peterson was sitting at one of the tables, talking to the young WPC, Gillian McKenzie.

'Constable McKenzie,' said Daykin, standing over them, 'haven't you got some house-to-house enquiries to look at?'

'Yes, sir,' she said, gulping down the last of her coffee and scuttling off as quickly as she could. But not so quickly that she couldn't give Toby Peterson a knowing smile.

If Daykin had been interested in Toby Peterson's love life he didn't get the chance to ask. The phone rang.

'A man called Andy on line two,' said Mavis.

'Hello, Andy, did you get the books?'

'My dad dropped them off yesterday.'

'I saw your name on the covers, did you do Michael Hilliam's accounts?'

'Yes, for about the last ten years.'

'Can you bring them up to date?'

'Who's paying?'

'North Yorkshire Constabulary.'

'Should take me about two days.'

'Do you know anything about the trips to France?'

Andy Liddle snorted.

'He wasn't still doing that, was he? I told him every time I gave him his accounts, I calculated it was costing him about ten thousand a year.'

'Could he afford a five star hotel in Nice?'

'He couldn't afford a meal at McDonald's.'

'Do you know his wife?'

'Charlotte Hilliam? No, thank God, only what I've heard. A cow of the first order. For ever giving him a hard time.'

'Thanks, Andy. Give me a call when you've finished the accounts. Give my best to Meg.'

There was a pause. Old friends never knew what to say to Tom Daykin about wives.

'See you, Tom.'

CHAPTER TWENTY

'I've phoned Ted Kenningham, he's looked at the van and he'll be here shortly,' said Daykin, looking at the piles of reports, intelligence summaries and computer sheets.

He sat down to read, using two cardboard boxes the photo-copying paper came in as in and out trays. The in tray was almost empty when the telephone beside him rang. He picked it up.

'Inspector Hyland for you, line one,' said Mavis, the tele-phone operator who always made an incoming call sound like a massive inconvenience. Daykin pushed the button with a small figure one in ballpoint pen written above it and turned on the speakerphone.

'Daykin.'

'Inspector Daykin, Bob Hyland from Kent Constabulary. I thought I'd see if you need anything else.'

'Is there CCTV footage of the entrance to the Channel Tunnel?'

'Of course, twenty-four hours a day.'

'Can you get someone to look for a blue Transit van if I send you the registration number and the approximate dates?'

'I've got a couple of constables who have been stepping a bit close to the line lately. They could do with a few days in front of a screen as punishment. Oh, and I've got some news for you.'

'What's that?'

'There is a local villain called Darren Hills who specializes in turning over houses while the owners are away. We caught him coming out of a window of one of those country houses with the silent alarms. Poor sod did not know we were there until I put a hand on his shoulder. Scared him to death. He had to admit to it at court and asked for twenty cases to be taken into consideration. One of them was this house.'

'Was it reported to the police?'

'Strangely, not.'

'Anything missing?'

'He says there wasn't anything worth taking. The wardrobe was half full of expensive clothes, but nothing saleable in the house at all. Before he left he did however look in the garage and guess what he found?'

'A dark-blue Transit van.'

'Exactly.'

'Thanks, Bob,' said Daykin and put the phone down.

'I don't understand, sir. Why was the blue Transit van in the garage at Ashford?' said Peterson.

'Do you remember the two petrol receipts from the same petrol station in Ashford? My guess is that he drove the blue Transit down from there and filled it up, ready for the trip back. Early the following morning he got the Mercedes Sprinter out of the garage, drove the Transit in and then took the Mercedes to the petrol station to fill it up before he went where he was going.'

'Where do you think he was going?'

'I hope that the next twenty-four hours will tell us, but my money would be on Paris.'

'Why Paris?'

'Later,' said Daykin. 'Let's get a cup of tea while we have the chance.'

They didn't get the chance. The water in the kettle was still rising towards boiling when Ted Kenningham walked in.

He had either joined the force very young or had lived a very clean life, because Ted Kenningham only looked about 40 years old. He was a tall man, just too broad to he called skinny, but slim without an ounce of excess fat. His hair, once blond, was now pure white and it flopped untidily across his forehead every time he moved. Under the hair, a ready smile broke out from an angular freckled face.

'I've fnished, Tom, and I have a few things for you,' he said in a broad Lancashire accent.

'Let's sit down,' said Daykin.

As soon as they were seated Ted Kenningham sat upright in his chair and turned his head from side to side, looking round the room like a meercat.

'Was that a kettle I heard boiling?' he asked.

Toby Peterson got slowly to his feet.

'I'll get it,' he said.

'One sugar, son,' said Kenningham.

He must be older than he looked. It was a while since anyone had called Toby Peterson 'son'.

'These will show you the full picture,' said Ted Kenningham, turning to Daykin.

He took a bundle of small clear plastic envelopes from his right-hand jacket pocket and spread them on the table, then he arranged them in a line.

'Let's start at the front of the vehicle,' he said, holding up an envelope containing a few blades of grass.

'From under the front bumper. That would indicate that he had driven on a road with grass on it, or over a field. I think the road because if it was a field I would expect a lot more grass, right across the bumper and under the wheel arches. So, a dirt road with a central line of grass on it, the sort of track that leads to a farmhouse.'

He put the envelope down on the table and picked up the next one. Daykin could only make out some purplish grey vegetation.

'Thistledown,' said Kenningham, 'from the front of the radiator. You do get dirt tracks in part of some cities, but you would not get this many thistles, so I am sure that he had been along a country dirt track some time recently.'

Toby Peterson returned with three mugs of tea as Ted Kenningham was picking up the next envelope.

'It's amazing.' he said, 'what the inside wall of a tyre can show. I pulled off the wheels and took some scrapings.'

He pushed the envelope across the table to Daykin.

'What does that tell you?'

Daykin looked at the contents of the envelope: five dried pieces of dirt.

'Not a lot,' he said, pushing the envelope back. He knew Ted did not get much chance to show off these days, so he acted as his straight man. 'What does it tell you?'

'That this vehicle drove through a muddy puddle at a slow speed and that the puddle wasn't in this area.'

'The soil varies from area to area,' continued Kenningham. 'This is clay-laden soil with low levels of loam from further south.'

He picked up another envelope.

'Two leaves caught in the trim on the side of the vehicle. I'm not sure and I'll have a botanist look at them, but I think they are larch.'

He picked up the last envelope.

'This is from the inside of the van. There were a few wood slivers, but you told me that the van carried furniture, so I thought you wouldn't be interested in those. Now this,' he said flicking the envelope with his finger so that the tiny off-white granules inside danced frantically, 'is far more interesting. This, gentlemen, is crack cocaine.'

'Are you sure?' asked Daykin.

'I had one of the drugs squad lads test it on his Noddy testing kit. Not good enough for a jury conviction, but enough so I'm sure.'

'Where's it from?'

'I'll come to that later. So,' he continued, 'what have we got? This van is carrying crack cocaine and has driven through a puddle on a dirt track with a central strip of grass near a larch tree. Any idea where that might be?'

Daykin knew it was his time for playing the straight man again.

'No,' he said, 'have you?'

'In the hills above Bradford.'

'Bradford!' said Toby Peterson. 'How the hell do you know that?'

It was a cheap trick but Ted Kenningham, when he was in the mood, was not above cheap tricks. From his left-hand jacket pocket, so it did not get mixed up with the others, he pulled out another clear plastic envelope. Inside it was a pay and display ticket.

'Norfolk Gardens multi-storey car-park, Central

Bradford,' he said, 'for two hours from 11.42 p.m. at night two months ago. They drove to Bradford, parked the van and met their buyers in a nightclub for a couple of drinks, then drove to a farmhouse to exchange the drugs and the money.'

'Bit risky, isn't it, leaving the van in a multi-storey car-park with drugs in it? They might have been stolen,' said Peterson.

'Not really. The van is old and battered enough so no one would want to steal it. And if they broke in they wouldn't find any drugs. They were in a hidden compartment welded under the passenger seat. That's where I found the crack cocaine.'

'Thanks, Ted,' said Daykin.

'I enjoyed it. I'll get the lads in Richmond to take care of the forensics and send you the results,' he said, and left. Ted Kenningham never had been one for goodbyes.

Daykin was silent for a long time. He polished his glasses, he stared out of the window, he drummed his fingers softly on the table. Toby Peterson didn't interrupt him, and went to make two more mugs of tea. When he got back to the table Daykin said, 'Tony Hammond is beginning to look more and more like a suspect, isn't he?'

Toby Peterson didn't quite follow, but he didn't want to say so, and kept silent.

'With just a bit more work, we can put him in a van with Michael Hilliam, delivering drugs to Bradford.'

'Why Bradford?'

'Most drugs in this country are delivered by road. The quickest way is by one of the motorways. More by accident than design, Bradford is at the junction of the M62 going east and west and the M1 going south. It's an ideal distribution centre. Drugs coming into the country at the ports of

Liverpool or Hull, or the airports, Liverpool, Manchester, Leeds/Bradford can be shipped to Bradford and from there anywhere down south. If you are wanting drugs to go from London up north, it's the same.'

'So we have him delivering drugs with Hilliam?'

'Yes, and Hilliam was killed in the church. They were the wardens, they both had keys to the church and we know that they met there some nights.'

'But if he was the killer and he had a key, why was the door forced?'

'It would look a bit obvious if it wasn't. That would mean either Michael Hilliam let his killer in late one night and what are the chances of that? Or it had to be the vicar, Mrs Sheppard or Tony Hammond. I don't think Hammond would want it to be a choice of three, the other two being a man of the cloth and a middle-aged woman.

'I've never believed that the door was forced,' he continued. 'To kill Michael Hilliam in that way you had to make plans and carry a knife. What was the killer going to do: make a very noisy break in, hoping that Hilliam would be there?

'I was missing two things: a motive and proof of the trip to Paris. The crack cocaine Ted found provided the motive, but for the theory I've got to hold water, Hammond had to go to France with Hilliam and he seems so confident that we can't show that he did.

'No. Let me think about it, I'm going to take the dog for a walk. I'll see you in my office in half an hour.'

As Daykin set off up the Moorland Road, the dog at his heels, Superintendent Jarvis watched him from his office window. Daykin was the devil for taking walks with his dog in the middle of the working day, but Jarvis let him do it

127

because he often came back from those walks with answers to difficult questions. He shrugged and went back to his desk to think about his next move on Paula Sykes.

CHAPTER TWENTY-ONE

DAYKIN, who had been sitting at his desk staring vacantly at the ceiling for twenty minutes, suddenly leaned forward.

'The van! Idiot! If Hilliam took the van to France once, he always took it!'

Toby Peterson and the dog sat up and looked at him in unison. The dog began to bark, woken up from his afternoon nap. Daykin glared at the dog and it stopped and settled itself back into the corner of the room.

'The van?' repeated Peterson.

'The burglar finds Hilliam not at home and the Transit in the garage, so he wasn't back in Yorkshire. So he must be in France and he's taken the Mercedes with him. If he took it then, he always took it, or he had no need for it. That's why Tony Hammond is so sure we wouldn't see him on CCTV at the Channel Tunnel. We'd be looking for the Transit and we'd never see it!'

'But why register the Mercedes in someone else's name?'

'At a guess, the someone whose name it is registered in has never met Hilliam and can't name or describe him. Supposing he was bringing drugs from France, hidden in antique furniture? He gets stopped by Customs. He tells them some story that he's just been told to deliver the van. Remember, he's still Jonathan Lister. They would almost certainly bail him for a few weeks while they made enquiries. They check his address in Ashford and that is OK. But what have they got if he doesn't come back? A photograph worth nothing, because he'll never use that disguise again. DNA and fingerprints that don't match to anyone with a criminal record and a van they can only trace to a woman who has never met him.'

'But Hammond, why did he have to go with Hilliam to France before he killed him?'

'Because he wanted to know what Hilliam knew,' said Daykin, reaching for the telephone.

'Get me Inspector Hyland, Mavis.'

'Who?'

You talked to him an hour ago.'

'He's not local, is he?'

'No, Mavis, he's with the Kent force.'

'Where he's stationed?'

'I don't know. Ring Ashford I think, they'll put you through to him.'

He put the telephone down. Mavis was getting worse, but she was an institution. He knew a retired uniform inspector who had served twenty-two years and claimed that after graduating police college and being assigned to this as his first station, Mavis was operating the telephones as if she'd been there for years.

Five minutes later, just when Daykin was about to pick up the telephone to remind her, it rang.

'Inspector Hyland on line one,' said Mavis, in the voice she put on when she wanted to sound harassed, 'and let me say, Inspector Daykin, I don't expect to have to chase all round the country for you again.'

Daykin would have told her that was actually her job, but Mavis had had years of practice of complaining, then cutting you off before you could reply. The telephone went dead. Daykin pushed button one.

'Tom Daykin,' he said.

'What can I do for you, Tom?'

'Those officers who are looking at the CCTV video, have they started yet?'

'From where I'm sitting, I can see them having a cup of tea, putting it off as long as possible.'

'I might have told you to look for the wrong vehicle. I don't think that they should be looking for the Transit: tell them to try the Mercedes that was in the garage at Ashford.'

'The white Sprinter?'

'That's the one. Do you have the registration number?'

'Just a minute.' There was a sound of rustling paper. 'Yes, I have it.'

'Thanks again, Bob.'

'I'll let you know when they tell me what they've found.'

Daykin put the telephone down and got up to his feet. The dog looked up at him expectantly. He shook his head and it put its head back on its front paws and closed its eyes, either sleeping or sulking.

'Let's contact the Child Protection Team,' said Daykin.

'Why?'

'Because our star witness, Red Malcolm, is in trouble and I need to know exactly how much trouble.'

He was going to ask Mavis to get him the number, but she was in one of her moods so he rang directory enquiries. When he got the number he was put through to a female detective called Ramsey.

'Do you have a file on a man called Malcolm Proctor?'

'Yes, why?'

'I know he's in trouble: I need to know what sort of trouble.'

'About three months ago the FBI raided some offices that were set up to take payments for access to an internet website. The website was child pornography. They only took credit card payments, so when the FBI went through the records, they could trace every subscriber. Malcolm had been paying regularly, now he's going to pay another way.'

'He's a potential witness of ours: can you put his file on the back burner for a few months?'

'I've got a pile of files on my desk, they all subscribed, they all went into the website and now they're all going to prison. No delays, no exceptions. Sir.'

They walked through the station back to the incident room.

'Tom Daykin,' said the custody sergeant, stirring his tea with a pencil, 'you've got a visitor.'

'What now, Harry?'

'Superintendent Jarvis was talking to him, but he seemed to want to wait in your office,' said the sergeant with a patronizing smile.

'Who is he?'

'A commander from Scotland Yard, no less.'

'What does he want?'

'Whatever it is, he won't tell Jarvis, so he won't tell the likes of me. He says he has something to discuss with you in confidence.'

The man in Tom Daykin's office was standing examining one of the pictures on the wall and had his back to the door as Daykin opened it. He had felt like knocking on his own office door, but decided against it. The man turned, hands behind his back, to look at Daykin as he came in. That gave Daykin the chance to look back and take stock of his visitor.

He was a tall man, well over six feet, dressed immaculately in a dark-blue business suit, white starched shirt, MCC tie, silk pocket handkerchief and above it on the lapel a small red buttonhole-rose.

'Inspector Daykin?' he said, stepping forward and offering his hand, 'Christopher Bennett.'

No rank and not the sign of anger at being kept waiting; this man was a class act.

'I've been keeping your dog company. May I sit down?'

Daykin walked round the desk and sat in his chair while Christopher Bennett seated himself opposite him.

'What can I do for you, Commander?' asked Daykin guardedly.

'It's Tony Hammond. I understand you have been investigating him. I'd like you to stop.'

By a bizarre twist of fate Daykin, who had just asked a junior officer to back away from her investigation, was now on the receiving end of the same request.

'Can I ask why?'

'I can't say.'

'I'm investigating Tony Hammond for conspiracy to import drugs, conspiracy to supply drugs and murder. If you can't say, I won't stop.'

'What if I give you a direct order?'

'I'll disobey it. You then take me to a disciplinary hearing and what you are trying to hide will all come out.'

Bennett looked at him with renewed interest before deciding that Daykin wasn't bluffing.

'His name is not Tony Hammond.'

'Go on.'

'It doesn't surprise me that you are investigating his

connection to drugs; it's in his past. About ten years ago he was part of an East London firm who were wholesaling drugs to all parts of the country. We raided them and caught some – including Tony – red handed. Then the witness intimidation started. Our case was falling apart, but we had Tony and a couple of the others on police officers' evidence alone, so he was looking at twenty years or more. We went to him with an offer: turn Queen's evidence against the big players and we'll look after you.'

'And he did?'

'As good as his word, we put three of the top boys away for life. We gave him a new identity and moved him to another part of the country.'

'Not here?'

'No, he hit a spot of local difficulty and we had to move him again. That's when we changed his identity for a second time and brought him up to North Yorkshire.'

'Local difficulty?'

'He knocked someone over and killed them. We couldn't risk a trial: his picture might get in the papers and someone might recognize him, so we covered it up and moved him.'

'And you think that if he faces a trial here, the same could happen?'

'That's about it. We've invested a lot of time and money in Tony Hammond and he's still giving us valuable information.'

'A farmhouse near Bradford?'

Christopher Bennett looked at him quizzically.

'No, he's not mentioned anything about that.'

'If, sir, he had told you about that, then he may have been simply working as a police informant. In that case, although I couldn't ignore what he may have done, I could soft peddle.

But I think that he is as guilty as hell of all the things I said. You and your department may have made him feel that he could do whatever he wants because he's too valuable for you to let him be put in front of a judge. He's about to learn one of the lessons of life: we all answer for our sins.'

'That's a pity, Inspector. You see, I can't let his identity become public.'

'Does Superintendent Jarvis know about this?' asked Daykin.

'You do things differently here. In the Witness Protection Scheme we only tell those people who have to know. I had to tell you, I don't have to tell the superintendent. Here is a direct order, you don't tell him anything about this conversation.

Commander Bennett got slowly to his feet and walked out of the room. This time he did not offer to shake hands.

CHAPTER TWENTY-TWO

THE inquest on Michael Hilliam had been formally opened and adjourned by the Coroner for further enquiries into the death. The only purpose of the short hearing was for the certificate to be issued, releasing the body for burial.

It was as if the weather knew that there was a funeral and wanted to add to the atmosphere. An hour before the short cortège of long black cars arrived, a rising west wind drove a bank of dark-grey thunder clouds across the sky and the rain, a heavy drizzle at first, turned into a steady downpour from a sky that was now uniformly grey from horizon to horizon.

For a man who in life appeared to have few friends, quite a crowd turned out to pay their respects to Michael Hilliam after his death. Daykin and Toby Peterson went to the funeral as observers, not mourners. They stood sheltering in the same lych gate that Robert Morton had paused in only a few days ago before going into the church and finding the body, setting in motion the chain of events that led to this funeral.

With hardly a sound, the hearse, followed by two black saloons, came round the corner at the far side of the High Street and drove at walking pace up the road towards them. The few people on the High Street stopped as the hearse passed, the old men taking off their caps and both men and women bowing their heads.

The hearse sighed to a stop in front of them and four young men dressed in identical black suits with identical solemn expressions on their faces, left the folding seats either side of the coffin and slid with practised ease from the back of the vehicle. Daykin had heard all the folklore about getting old when police officers look young, but the real test was when undertakers looked young. These four men looked very young to him. He guessed that this was a family business and that they were taught to look solemn before they were in their teens.

With trained precision, the coffin was slid out of the back of the hearse and lifted on to four shoulders. It was carried in a slow march through the lych gate and along the cobbled path to the newly repaired church door, where they paused. Michael Hilliam was about to go through a funeral service and then be buried yards from where he had died.

Perhaps Daykin would have fallen into line with the rest of the mourners and filed into the church behind the coffin, but the memories of walking behind his wife's coffin into another country church and crying tears that fell into her grave were too fresh, too painful. He decided to wait outside. He looked for somewhere to shelter nearer the church. Then he saw him.

Twenty yards away, leaning forward, his arms folded across the top of the spade's handle, one foot resting on the top of the blade, was the sexton, Trevor Wilkins. He stood beside the open grave he had spent the last two hours digging: there was no emotion in his eyes as he watched the mourners. He had seen it all a hundred times before.

'If you want to know what has gone on in a church, don't ask the vicar or the parish council, ask the sexton,' said

Daykin quietly to Toby Peterson, and set off to walk across the freshly mown grass of the graveyard. He stopped when he was standing beside Trevor Wilkins.

'Morning, Trevor,' he said.

'Mr Daykin,' acknowledged Wilkins. Except for his mouth, no part of his body – not even his eyes – moved. He seemed oblivious to the rain that ran in tiny rivers down his wax jacket and dripped constantly from the peak of his sodden flat cap.

'Sad business,' said Daykin.

'Aye, no one should go like that.'

'If you were me,' said Daykin, 'who would you put your money on?'

'That Malcolm Proctor's got too much ambition for his own good,' replied Trevor Wilkins, nodding at the line of mourners at the church door and sending a spray of droplets of water from the peak of his cap. Daykin looked at the door of the church and could just see the back of Proctor as he went into the building, taking off his dark-blue cap. He was wearing a black tie and a dark blue suit but he couldn't resist the red anorak.

'What makes you say that?' he asked.

'He's always wanted to be senior churchwarden, made no secret of it and was pissed off when Michael Hilliam got it. Well, now it's open to him again, so he'll be buttering up the vicar.'

'Doesn't the junior churchwarden automatically become senior warden?'

'No, it's in the vicar's gift. Michael Hilliam was not junior churchwarden before he got the job as senior warden.'

'I see,' said Daykin, although it was just something to say. 'Thanks, Trevor, you've given me something to think about.'

'Any time, Mr Daykin,' said Trevor Wilkins, who had still not looked at Daykin once.

Daykin walked back to where Toby Peterson was sheltering under the lych gate roof.

'Anything useful, sir?'

'Just another finger, pointing at Malcolm Proctor this time.'

They didn't move until the coffin was carried back out of the church and the solemn, silent procession marched slowly to the graveside. Daykin and Peterson walked to join the back of the circle of people standing round the rectangular hole in the dark earth.

At the head of the grave, the Reverend Morton recited the liturgy as the four young men from the hearse took the strain on two canvas belts passed under the coffin and slowly and patiently lowered it into the ground. Without a pause, Morton picked up a handful of earth.

'Earth to earth, ashes to ashes,' he shouted loudly and dramatically into the wind and threw the earth into the grave.

Daykin shuddered. There was nothing more haunting or more final than the sound of earth falling on to a coffin lid.

'Let's go,' he whispered to Toby Peterson, and they silently stole away from the burial. By now the falling rain made the only sound in the graveyard.

'So Tony Hammond is not the only one who could be the killer?' asked Toby Peterson as they got into the car.

'I still think that he's the most likely, but we'd better take a look at Proctor. Why don't you make a few phone calls, see if anyone else thinks the same as Trevor Wilkins.

'Take the car if you want,' he continued, passing the keys to Peterson.

'Where are you going, sir?'

'To The Feathers, I'll give you a call when I'm finished.'

Daykin walked to The Feathers. It had struck him as odd that he hadn't seen Tony Hammond, the man everyone said was Michael Hilliam's best friend, at the burial service.

The rain had stopped, but there was still a stiff breeze blowing along the High Street. The weather was just bad enough to keep the numbers in The Feathers down to single figures. Tony Hammond stood alone at the bar, wiping the beer-engine handles with a damp cloth. He was wearing an expensive sweater and a cold smile. Daykin leaned across the bar so he could speak quietly and be heard only by Hammond.

'I had a visitor yesterday.'

Tony Hammond looked at him nodding but saying nothing. He knew what Daykin was talking about.

'He warned me not to ask questions about you.'

Hammond had stopped wiping the handles and put the cloth on the bar. He leant towards Daykin, so that their faces almost touched.

'And what did you say?'

Something in his voice made it more a threat than a question.

'I told him,' said Daykin slowly, 'to sod off.'

'Some people, people with more clout than a country bobby, would say that that was a stupid thing to do.'

'You might think that you can do what you want and those who protect you will spirit you away. You need to know that if you've done anything wrong, they can't protect you from the law and they can't protect you from me. I will nail you.'

Daykin would never know if it was disbelief or bravado, but Tony Hammond simply smiled and picked up the cloth again.

'We'll see.'

Tony Hammond had nothing more to say, but Daykin's

timing was good because at that moment the other man he wanted to see, Malcolm Proctor, walked in and ordered a pint of beer. Daykin waited for him to sit down on the padded bench against the far wall and then slid in beside him.

'Malcolm,' he said without any introduction, 'where were you last Tuesday night?'

Malcolm Proctor took a drink from his glass.

'Last Tuesday, Mr Daykin? The night of the murder? I was at home all evening.'

'What did you do?'

'From when?'

'Why not start at about eight o'clock?'

'Let me see' – another sip of beer – 'I took the dog for a walk at about seven thirty, got home about twenty past eight. I had a bath and came downstairs at maybe ten past nine. Yes it was, because a film had just started. I watched that until it finished at eleven, then went to bed.'

'What was the film?'

'To tell you the truth. I was really tired that evening and the film wasn't very good. I didn't enjoy it, but had to see how it ended. I couldn't tell you what it was called.'

'What was it about?'

'I didn't realize it would be important; I spent more time dozing off than watching it.'

'If you are lying to me, and I think you may be, then you and I will have another talk,' said Daykin as he got up to leave.

As he walked out of the bar he could feel Malcolm Proctor's eyes on his back and he and Tony Hammond exchanged glares. Daykin decided that he would not be the winner of any popularity contests in The Feathers.

CHAPTER TWENTY-THREE

IT was midmorning on the follwing day that Inspector Hyland called Daykin from Kent.

'The boys tell me that every date you've given us shows the Mercedes Sprinter going through the Channel Tunnel.'

'What about the last time?'

'That's a bit more difficult, the man you described with dark hair and designer glasses got out to stretch his legs. You can see that he had a passenger, but you can't see through the windscreen who it is.'

'No description at all?'

'From the size, you can say that it is almost certainly a man and that he's wearing a white shirt or sweater, but that's about all you can say.'

'It might well be enough,' replied Daykin. 'Thanks, Bob. I owe you one.'

'Next time you're in Kent why don't you buy me a pint?'

'Why not say next time you're in Yorkshire I'll buy you a pint. The beer's better.'

After he put the telephone down he took the dog for a walk and when he came back he and Toby Peterson drove to Asquith. The sale in Hilliam's Antiques was not producing a football match crowd of people and winding up the estate may well take some time, which didn't seem to bother Mrs Potterton.

'Can we take another look round the shop?' asked Daykin.

She was happy for the company and went off to make them a cup of tea.

'What are we looking for?' asked Toby Peterson.

'The SOCO team went over Michael Hilliam's house with a fine-tooth comb. I'm sure that he was dealing drugs and that's why he was killed. If there were any drugs at his house the SOCO's would have found them.'

'Crime Scene Investigators.'

'What?'

'Crime Scene Investigators, that's what they call themselves these days, sir.'

'What happened to SOCO?'

'American television.'

'Whatever they call themselves, they didn't find any drugs at the house. He had to store them somewhere, which means his house or his shop, and we know it's not the house.'

He looked round the shop.

'There's something here, I can feel it.'

'What if we don't find anything?'

'Then I have to have a major rethink.' Daykin paused. 'What have you had for breakfast that makes you ask all these questions?'

'Shall we just get on with it, sir?' said Toby Peterson, convinced that they were wasting their time.

Two hours and three mugs of tea later, Daykin was beginning to agree with him. They had knocked on walls, stamped on floors and borrowed a ladder to get into the space under eaves. There was no sign that this was anything but an antique shop. Then, standing in the office doorway, Daykin downed the last of his third mug of tea and looked distractedly into the office.

'Toby,' he said slowly, turning his head to one side, 'come and look at this.'

Toby Peterson stood beside him and followed his line of sight.

'I can't see what you're looking at, sir.'

'This wall by the window, it's about six inches further forward than the other one.'

'Perhaps that's just the way the place was built.'

'Let's take a really good look at it, just to be sure.'

When they eventually found it, it was beautifully designed and constructed. A real work of art, probably based on secret drawers Hilliam had seen in antique writing desks. What looked like a small knot of wood in the skirting board when pressed, revealed a tiny metal handle that shot out on a spring. When the handle was pulled, the bottom four rows of bricks, three bricks wide, slid out on polished metal rollers which moved silently on rows of ball-bearings. Inside the space was a package about the size of a bag of flour, wrapped in cling film and sealed with brown packaging tape.

'I'll get a drugs bag from the car,' said Toby Peterson.

He came back with a self-sealing bag and a pair of latex gloves. He pulled the gloves on, then gently lifted the package into the bag and sealed and labelled it. Then he looked into the space behind the false wall. It could store about twenty packages.

'Wouldn't you expect more than one package, sir?'

'They'd just come back from a trip to Bradford. My guess is that this package was a reserve, just in case of emergencies, the rest have already been delivered.'

A short statement was taken from Mrs Potterton, to say that she knew nothing about the false wall in the office and they drove back to the station where the package was locked in the drugs cupboard.

Mrs Potterton watched them walk away down the High Street. She reached for the phone and dialled a number.

'Charlotte? You said to call you if the police came here; they've just left. No, two of them, the fat inspector and that young sergeant. They were here for quite a while. They took a bag away with them after they found a hiding place in one of the walls. No, I don't know what was in the bag. Yes, I'll let you know if they come back.'

She put the phone down and smiled to herself. They were all fools, Charlotte most of all.

When he got back in his office Daykin decided to speak to Commander Bennett. He discovered just how difficult it was for a country inspector to speak to a Scotland Yard commander. He was routed through department after department and assistant after assistant, each telling him that they could take a message. If it hadn't been so important he would have given up after fifteen minutes, but finally his patience was rewarded.

'Bennett,' said a voice at the end of the telephone.

'Tom Daykin, sir, about Tony Hammond.'

'I'm not talking about this over the telephone.'

'I just need two pieces of information. I don't want to travel to London for a five-minute conversation.'

'No need, I'll be coming to Yorkshire very soon.'

'To take care of things?'

'I can't let you arrest him; you know why.' There was a pause. 'You haven't arrested him, have you?'

'No, sir, but now I have all the proof I need.'

'Arresting him will make my job very difficult.'

'The information I wanted, sir?'

'If I give it to you, no arrest?'

'You know I can't do that, sir. I have to make the arrest.'

'I'll tell you what I will do, I will give you the information. It doesn't really matter much now: events will take care of themselves.'

'Thank you, sir. Was Tony Hammond ever in the services?'

'Odd question, but the answer is yes. Royal Marines. He was dishonourably discharged, something about breaking into the quartermaster's stores and selling off stolen goods to the locals. Next question.'

'Before he moved to Yorkshire, exactly where was he living?'

'Just outside Birmingham.'

'Exactly?'

'Warmley Road, Edgbaston,' he said with a sigh of exasperation. 'That's your two questions, Inspector,' and he put the telephone down.

Down the corridor Mark Jarvis picked up the phone and dialled an internal number. While he waited for it to be answered he pulled two tickets he had just bought out of his pocket and looked at them.

'Paula?' he said, forgetting their agreement, 'I've been given two tickets for the theatre in Richmond tonight, would you care to go with me?'

It had been a long day, but Daykin leaned back in his chair and reflected on what a good day it had been. He had solved the case, now all he had to do was to arrest Tony Hammond, talk him into making a full confession and close the file.

'Time to go home, Toby,' he said.

'Aren't you going to arrest Tony Hammond, sir?'

Daykin thought about it many times later and didn't know if he was tired, if he couldn't face two late nights in a row, or whether Commander Bennett's words made him delay things until the morning.

'No, he'll keep until first thing tomorrow. Meet me here at seven thirty and we'll go and pick him up. That will give us a full day to interview him.'

CHAPTER TWENTY-FOUR

HE was running through a field of poppies, an ocean of red flower heads as far as he could see. Behind him were dark clouds, moving quickly across the sky and dropping a curtain of heavy drops of rain. He ran, but the clouds were gaining on him. Then he heard ringing. It came from a bright yellow telephone box in the middle of the field. He ran towards it, but it kept moving away from him.

Slowly, very slowly, he came out of the dream. The telephone on his bedside table was ringing. He looked at the numbers on the digital alarm clock. Two minutes past six. In the darkness he reached for the telephone.

'Yes,' he said, his voice still thick with sleep.

'Toby Peterson, sir. I think you'd better meet me at the station as soon as you can get here.'

'Why, what's going on?'

'It's Tony Hammond, sir. He's dead.'

Daykin showered, shaved, dressed and drove to the station at record speed, all the time trying to get his head round the fact that Tony Hammond was dead. Had he misjudged the facts from start to finish? Had he got it completely wrong?

The incident room door was locked, so he raced across the car-park and through the back door of the station, the dog, following him at a jog, thinking this was some new game.

Toby Peterson was in the charge office waiting for him.

'When, where and how?' Daykin asked in disbelief.

'Exactly the same as Michael Hilliam, sir.'

'If you've got the keys, let's go to the incident room.'

On their way down the corridor, Chief Inspector Sykes stopped them.

'What's this I hear about your prime suspect being stabbed?'

'Sergeant Pullan has just explained to me what a mess this is, ma'am.'

'Well, see if you can sort it out and you'd better do it quickly.'

Toby Peterson had had the good sense to get all the officers involved in the Hilliam murder to the incident room.

'If anybody has got this wrong. it's me. Now I need your help, and it's going to take a lot of mind-numbing, boring drudgery. I want house-to-house, revisiting every house on the original enquiry, asking if they saw anything last night or anything that was the same last night as it was on the night of Michael Hilliam's murder. Give Tony Hammond's house a good going over, get a search team in from Richmond if you have to. Tell them to go through The Feathers thoroughly, and not just the areas you think he had access to.'

Daykin turned to Toby Peterson.

'Toby, what about the SOCO and Forensics?'

'The Crime Scene Investigation team are already there and the pathologist is on his way.'

'Who discovered him?'

'A routine mobile patrol passed the church at about four

this morning and saw what he thought was a light in the church. He went to take a look and it was the mirror image of Michael Hilliam's murder, just a different body.'

'What do you mean?'

'The church door had been forced, the body was in exactly the same position with the same wounds.'

'Same cause of death?'

'The pathologist will tell you for sure, but I'd say yes.'

'The light?'

'That's the only thing that's different, it's as if someone wanted the body found as quickly as possible. The vestry light had been left burning.'

Daykin looked round the table.

'You guys know what you have to do, get on with it. Toby, let's take a look at the church.'

In the car on the way to Camleigh, Daykin said, 'Why did it take two hours to contact me?'

'The officer who found the body radioed into the station and the sergeant on duty called me. I wanted to make sure of my facts, so I drove in and talked to the officer. Then I called the Crime Scene Investigators, the pathologist's department and I left a message at the coroner's office.'

Revd Morton hadn't tried to clean the carpet where Michael Hilliam had died, he had paid for it to be removed and replaced with a new one. The substituted carpet, twelve feet long down the nave and six feet wide into the transepts, had been of the same make and colour but, being newer, was lighter. Not now though, it was saturated with the dark blood that oozed round the body of Tony Hammond.

He lay in exactly the same position as Michael Hilliam, the same vacant expression frozen on his lifeless face that stared up at the church ceiling twenty feet above him. Or was there something else in the expression? Daykin couldn't be sure. The arms were spread straight out as if in crucifixion, the shoes and socks had been removed and laid neatly to one side, the socks tucked into the shoes. It was as if someone, having brutally killed him, was now all tenderness and care.

And the gaping wounds appeared the same at first sight. One in each of his hands and feet where an instrument had been pushed right through the flesh. As Daykin looked closer, he saw the dried blood that had seeped from each of the wounds.

There was a bright flash from the doorway. Daykin turned to look. It was the photographer, taking pictures of the broken wood round the door lock.

'Have you finished with the body?' called Daykin across the near empty church.

'All yours,' shouted the photographer, without turning round to see who was calling him.

The pathologist came out of the vestry where, Daykin guessed, there was a sink and he had washed his hands after taking off the latex gloves.

'You took your time getting here, Tom,' he said.

Daykin looked down at the body of Tony Hammond again.

'Same as before?' he asked.

The pathologist knelt beside the body and motioned Daykin to kneel down at the other side.

'Not quite; see these marks,' he said, pointing with the ball-point pen he had taken from his pocket to a series of fine dark red lines running round the head in a thick band, both above and below the mouth.

'That,' said the pathologist, 'was where a gag was placed round his mouth.' He turned the head to one side, so the back was facing Daykin.

'That was after this blow on the head to knock him uncon-scious,' he said, pointing to a lump that was just visible below the close-cropped hair.

'Why was he gagged?'

'I'll show you.'

The pen pointed to both wrists in turn. Similar marks, but deeper in colour and narrower.

'His hands were tied with rope before he died. Then the gag and the rope were removed after death.'

'Why would anyone do that?'

'Because,' said the pathologist, pointing to each of the hand and foot wounds in turn, 'these were caused before he died. Someone pierced his hands and feet with a knife, then stabbed him through the heart. Someone wanted him to die as painfully as possible.'

'That's why these wounds seeped blood?'

'I do believe you'll make a pathologist yet,' said Dr Caisley as he got to his feet.

'Do I have to wait for a report?'

'You can do, but you now know ninety-nine per cent of what it will say. I'll give you a call if anything surprising comes up.'

'Hello, Tom,' said a voice from behind Daykin. He turned.

'Morning, Phil,' he said to Sergeant Carter, 'are you the SOCO?'

'Yep,' said Carter looking down at the body. 'Déjà vu.'

'It looks like it. Found anything so far?'

'He was knocked unconscious somewhere near the door and dragged over here, see those marks on the carpet? Those are his heel marks. Then he was bound and gagged, his shoes and socks removed and the knife put through his hands and feet. The pain of that would have woken him up. Then a single stab through the heart to end it all.'

'Dr Caisley says he would have died in some pain.'

'I'd say so. Someone wanted him to suffer before he died.'

'Why?'

'That's not my problem, Tom, it's yours.'

Phil Carter looked round the church.

'Nice place, seems peaceful enough. Who would want to kill both churchwardens?'

'If I could answer that Phil, I wouldn't be standing here. I'd be out arresting someone.'

'We've got about another hour here, Tom,' said Sergeant Carter, nodding to three men on their hands and knees, searching round the altar under the harsh glare of arc lamps. 'If we find anything I'll give you a bell.'

Daykin turned to Toby Peterson.

'Let's head back to the station, there must be a thousand forms to fill in.'

They walked down the nave of the church and had turned towards the door when it opened suddenly, almost knocking over the white-suited Crime Scenes Investigation Officer who was examining the shattered woodwork round the lock. Robert Morton came through the door and stopped to look at the strange scene in the interior of his church. The usual muted lighting was now pools of brilliant pale light and what was usually the congregation were ghostly figures in white suits. Then there was the body. It was just as he had been told, his worst nightmare. The man he had appointed to be senior warden only yesterday, lying on his new carpet in exactly the same perverted crucifixion pose as poor Michael Hilliam. This time he didn't feel like vomiting and realized with more than a little horror, that he was becoming immune to dead, crucified bodies appearing in his church.

'Vicar?' said Daykin.

Revd Morton looked at him and shook his head.

'This can't be happening again, Inspector.'

'I'm afraid it has. Are you all right to talk?'

Robert Morton gave an involuntary shudder. What was the old saying? Someone had just walked over my grave? How apt, he thought.

'Yes, of course, Inspector, anything I can do to help.'

Daykin looked round the church.

'Why not the choir stalls. It's brighter up there.'

They sat side by side. Toby Peterson directly behind them, in choir stalls placed in the church when it was built in the late Victorian era, when more people went to church. No choir had sung here for over fifty years and probably never would again.

'What can you tell me about Tony Hammond?' asked Daykin gently, as Robert Morton vacantly watched the undertakers wrap the body, place it on a guéridon and silently and slowly wheel it out of the church. He waited until they had closed the door behind them before he spoke, as if what he was about to say might offend Tony Hammond.

'You see, Inspector,' he began, 'I didn't really know Tony all that well, he'd only lived in the village for two years, but he was a real live wire.'

'How do you mean, exactly?'

'He came to the church and started suggesting fundraising events. He organized a charity auction and acted as auctioneer. He was terribly good and I think we raised over a thousand pounds. Then he got himself elected to the council, although, I must confess, we have more places than applicants. He took the chair of the fundraising committee and when Mr Taylor retired as junior churchwarden, I thought I would ask Tony, as he seemed so involved in the life of the church.'

'Was he stepping on anyone's toes?'

'Oh, I think there are a number of people who would like to be called churchwarden, but the only person I actually heard sounding off was Malcolm Proctor.'

'What did he say?'

'I can't remember now, but I know that he was disappointed when Michael Hilliam was appointed senior churchwarden. I rather think that he thought that the next appointment would definitely be him.'

'Anybody else?'

Revd Morton thought for a moment.

'No one I can think of, in fact, to the contrary. Everyone in the village seemed to like him. Those who don't go to church go down to The Feathers so everyone met him at one time or another. No, no enemies. . . .' His voice trailed off as he could see what a stupid thing it was to say. Someone had just stabbed Tony Hammond to death.

'Tell me about Malcolm Proctor,' said Daykin.

Toby Peterson, who was putting his notebook away, took it out again.

'Malcolm? He's harmless enough. A bit odd in some ways, I suppose, but a good enough soul.'

'What do you mean, a bit odd?'

'Nothing really. He doesn't seem to have any friends, spends a lot of time alone.' He smiled. 'Then of course, there's that dreadful red anorak.'

'Anything else you can tell us?'

'There are those, and may I say I've never seen any evidence of it, who say that he drinks and smokes too much, but that might just be loneliness. And he can't enjoy a drink too much anyway.'

'Why not?'

'Apparently he has some rare disease, it's not life threatening, but it has taken away nearly all his taste. He can only taste the basics of sweet and sour.'

'Riveting,' said Toby Peterson quietly.

Daykin shot him a look.

'Well, Vicar, we've taken enough of your time, we'll let you get on with what you are doing,' said Daykin.

The two policemen walked out of the now-deserted church, leaving the Vicar sitting in the choir stalls staring morosely at the large dark pattern of blood staining his new carpet.

CHAPTER TWENTY-FIVE

D AYKIN'S fear of completing mountains of forms was exaggerated, but not by much. He and Peterson spent the rest of the morning and well into the afternoon paper pushing until Daykin got tired of it.

'Let's go and see Malcolm Proctor,' he said.

Malcolm Proctor was a man who lived, like Robert Morton, by routine. They didn't need to make an appointment to see him, they had a good idea where he would be. By the time they arrived in the village he would be preparing his tea, usually something fried, or fish fingers on Fridays with doorsteps of buttered bread and a large mug of tea, three sugars.

Daykin opened the rusty wrought-iron gate that hung precariously to its post by one mangled hinge. They walked down the unswept path between overgrown lawns and flowerbeds that were mainly weeds, to a badly painted front door. Daykin pushed the bell. He was an optimist, it didn't work. He didn't want to risk his knuckles on the flaking paintwork, so he turned around and kicked the door three times with the heel of one of his size eleven shoes. They could just hear a radio playing at the back of the house. It grew softer, as if someone had turned down the volume, not sure if he had heard something, so Daykin kicked the door again. The radio went silent and they could hear shuffling along the hallway, the sound growing louder as it came towards the door. The front door opened, it was not locked, and the face of Malcolm Proctor stared at them through the two-inch gap.

'Remember me, Malcolm?' said Daykin pleasantly.

The sight of two police officers made Malcolm Proctor open the door, although he opened it slowly.

'Come in, Mr Daykin,' he said, turning his back as he retreated down the hallway. The shuffling sound started again, he was wearing an ancient pair of carpet slippers at least three sizes too large for him.

As they went through the front door, the first thing they saw was a concertina plastic coat rack hammered on to the wall by two six-inch nails. On it hung a red anorak.

'Thank God for that,' muttered Daykin, 'I thought he slept in it.'

They followed Malcolm Proctor to the kitchen at the end of the hallway. It was a hygienist's nightmare: the counter tops and floor thick with grease, the cooker unloved and uncleaned for years, empty tins everywhere and the prevailing smell of fried food which seemed to stick to the back of Daykin's throat.

'Sit down, Mr Daykin,' said Malcolm Proctor, pulling a plastic-coated chair from under the formica top table. Daykin looked at the chair and thought about the dry-cleaning bill.

'No thanks, Malcolm, I'll stand.'

'What do you want?' asked Proctor, already annoyed that his routine of tea at the stroke of five o'clock was being disturbed.

'Where were you last night?'

'Not again!'

'Yes, again.'

'Haven't you heard about Tony Hammond's death?' asked Toby Peterson.

Malcolm Proctor looked at him with disdain.

'In a village this size? Of course I've heard of it, I probably heard before you did.'

There was something in his expression that Daykin had seen before, it looked like smugness.

'I stayed in and watched television,' he said, looking at them both in turn.

'Really?'

'I can tell you what programmes I watched.'

'You could have videoed them and watched them later,' said Toby Peterson.

'I don't have a video recorder and I don't know how to use one.'

'Tell me what you watched,' said Daykin.

'From when?'

'Start at nine o'clock.'

'I saw the start of the news on One, then switched over because I remembered that there was a film on Five from nine to eleven. After that, I made myself a cup of tea and went to bed.'

'Alone?' said Daykin. He had to ask the question, but everyone in the room already knew the answer.

'Yes. I was asleep by eleven thirty.'

'So no alibi?'

'Anything else you can tell us?' asked Toby Peterson.

'All I can say, Mr Daykin, is that I haven't killed anyone.'

At the station they walked back to the incident room. It was empty.

'Where is everyone?' asked Daykin.

'Gone home, sir.'

Daykin stretched.

'It's getting late, why don't you follow them?'

'See you in the morning, sir.'

CHAPTER TWENTY-SIX

DAYKIN sat at a table in the incident room, wading methodically through the papers in front of him. He took off his glasses and rubbed his eyes, then squinted at his watch. It was 9.30, even a Scotland Yard commander should be in his office by now. He picked up the phone.

'See if you can get me Commander Bennett at Scotland Yard, will you?'

'Scotland Yard in London?'

'There's only one, Mavis.'

He put his glasses on and went back to his paperwork until the phone rang.

'Commander Bennett, line one.'

Daykin pushed the button on the phone.

'Have you got five minutes, Commander?'

'For what?'

'A few questions about Tony Hammond.'

'You're going to ask me if I had him killed?'

That was impressive, Bennett knew before Jarvis.

'Did you?'

'Don't be stupid, Inspector. I don't order people to be

161

killed. And if I did, do you really think I'd leave the body lying around?'

'I had to ask.'

'I suppose you did,' said Bennett and put the phone down. He was not a man for social niceties.

Toby Peterson walked into the incident room.

'Anything new sir?' he asked.

'No surprises. We won't be arresting anyone from Scotland Yard. How about you?'

'The house-to-house produced nothing, and they're nearly finished. Twenty officers did a fingertip search of the grave-yard today. Again, nothing. Unless you count twenty-eight pence in coins, three empty cigarette packets and a used condom.'

'In the graveyard?'

'Some people have weird ideas of places to have fun.'

'Anything from the SOCO?'

'Only one thing, they found a piece of broken shoelace under one of the pews near the aisle.'

'When was the church last cleaned?'

'I don't know.'

'That can wait for now. What does the pathologist say?'

'Post-mortem eleven tomorrow morning. You want to go?'

'No, I've seen enough for one month. You?'

'I'll pass, thanks, sir.'

'Someone has to go, send one of the CID officers first thing tomorrow.'

'The passport arrived this morning.'

'Good. Get some colour copies and send them by overnight courier to Inspector Labrun in Cannes and Sergent Dupont in Paris. Ask the inspector to show the photograph to Yvette Benastre, tell him to keep the questions neutral, but let's see if she identifies Jonathan Lister.

'The Paris job is more complicated,' he continued. 'Have you got the registration number of the white Mercedes van?'

Peterson nodded.

'Ask the sergent to see if the van was parked in the Porte de Vanves area on the days Lister was in the South of France. Tell him to concentrate on the antique dealers.'

'Why antique dealers?'

'Because Porte de Vanves is full of them. Hilliam's plan wouldn't work without one of them filling the van with antiques.'

'You still think Hammond killed him?'

'It would be nice to solve one murder in this case.'

CHAPTER TWENTY-SEVEN

'WHO has gone to the post-mortem?' asked Daykin as he came through the door of the incident room.

'Reynolds,' said Peterson.

'Reynolds? He can't pass a butcher's window without fainting.'

'Harvey said he had a lot of paperwork to do.'

'Then he gets the next one. We have a cleaner to see.'

He went to the nearest telephone and picked it up.

'Mavis, can you get Revd Morton on the line, he's the priest at the church where the murders took place.'

'I know who he is, I read the papers.'

Three minutes later the same telephone rang.

'It's the vicar,' said Mavis, 'line two.'

Daykin pressed the button.

'Mr Morton?'

'It's the modern way to call the Vicar by his first name, I think we know each other well enough by now, call me Robert.'

Daykin felt that, in his heart of hearts, Robert Morton did not approve of being called by his first name, so he didn't rush to do it.

'The church,' he began, 'who cleans it and how often?'

The question must have taken Robert Morton by surprise.

'There's a rota organized by the Mother's Union. They take it in turns to clean the church every Thursday afternoon.'

'So the church was cleaned the day before the body was discovered?'

'I believe so.'

'Who did the cleaning?'

'Just a minute, I think I have the rota here somewhere.'

Daykin heard papers being shuffled and guessed that Robert Morton was rummaging through the untidy paperwork that littered the desk in his study. There was a muffled grunt of satisfaction and the vicar came back on the telephone.

'Let's see,' he began, looking down the list of names, 'ah, yes. Mrs Cheetham and Mrs Flynn.'

'Do you have telephone numbers for them?'

'Yes, I have them here on the rota.'

Daykin took down the two telephone numbers and, thanking the vicar for his help, he hung up.

He pressed another button on the telephone and called the first of the two numbers.

'Post Office,' said a female voice.

Daykin was taken aback for a second.

'Mrs Cheetham?' he asked.

'Yes.' she said, 'who is that?'

'Inspector Daykin, North Yorkshire Police.'

'What can I do for you, Inspector?'

'I believe that you and Mrs Flynn cleaned the church on Thursday?'

'No.'

'No?'

'Mrs Flynn was not well. I cleaned the church on my own.'

'Can I come to speak to you?'

'How long will it take, I'm very busy.'

'About an hour.'

'Today?'

'I'd prefer it.'

'When?'

'I can be there in thirty minutes.'

'I take it that it's urgent.'

'It is.'

She sighed. 'I'll see you in half an hour.'

Daykin put the telephone down and turned to Toby Peterson.

'I'm going to see Mrs Cheetham about the church, I should be about two hours. Did you organize the copy passport going to Paris and the South of France, Toby?'

'Yes, sir.' said Toby Peterson. 'I'll keep on at the uniforms; they should finish the routine stuff today. DC Reynolds is on his way to the post-mortem and Harvey is correlating the paperwork. Anything else?'

'I don't think so, I'll see you in a couple of hours.'

He had allowed time for the journey in case sheep or agricultural traffic blocked the roads, but there were none and he arrived in the village within twenty minutes. He parked the car and took the dog for a stroll along the High Street. He kept it off the leash and it stayed at his heel and when they returned to the car, got quickly back into it, as if it knew that if it behaved itself there was another walk to be had later.

Mrs Margaret Cheetham was the postmistress and was behind the counter when Daykin walked in to the post office. He opened the door and an old brass bell on a spring rang. It seems that most of the shops in Camleigh had them. The post office, a counter behind three glass screens, was at the far end of the shop. The rest of the interior had been a stationery shop but the national chains that sold books, magazines, compact discs, greetings cards and stationery had eaten into its business and it now was clinging on, selling anything it could, including brown boxes of vegetables under a handwritten sign, 'local organic produce'. And a large rack of cards containing screws, nails, hooks and picture hooks. Mr Liddle would not be pleased if he knew.

In truth, despite what she said on the telephone, Mrs Cheetham did not look very busy. Apart from Daykin, there was nobody else in the shop. He walked up to the post office counter and produced his warrant card.

'Mrs Cheetham? Inspector Daykin.'

He passed the card across the counter under the glass screen where it was examined very briefly before she passed it back to him.

'If this is going to take some time, you'd better come upstairs.'

She opened a door behind her and called up the stairs.

'George, can you come down and mind the counter for a while?'

Daykin listened to the chronology of George's journey. There was a muffled mumbling and the sound of ancient springs as someone levered themselves off a sofa. Sliding sounds as a pair of slippers skated across the carpet, moving but never leaving the surface, like cross-country skis. Then the soft-padded footsteps as he came carefully down the steep steps that led to the door she had just opened. Daykin had a mental impression of George in his mind before he came into view, and he was not far wrong. As George came down the stairs, he appeared from the feet up. A pair of battered tartan-felt carpet slippers, grey-flannel trousers, a beige cardigan with leather buttons over a mid-grey open-necked shirt and a lean, lined face with clear brown eyes and sandy hair matching the pair of wild, untamed eyebrows. The face looked at him from behind thin wisps of smoke rising from a large briar pipe.

'Put that pipe out, George,' demanded Mrs Cheetham.

George, deprived of the twin comforts of peace and his pipe within a minute, looked at her with what would, years ago, have been the fires of anger, but was now only the ashes of resignation. He pulled a bright blue clay ashtray, 'A Present from Truro' in white script, from under the counter and gently tapped the pipe out.

'I'll be upstairs if anyone needs me,' said Mrs Cheetham and they left George to stand guard over an empty shop.

The stairs were dangerously steep, the flight going almost vertically upwards with a sharp right-hand curve at the top and without the safety net of a handrail. Margaret Cheetham, with years of experience to guide her, moved up them with the speed and sure tread of a mountain goat. Following her, Daykin was slower and more careful.

The living-room at the top of the stairs could have been moved in its entirety into a museum. Nothing in it was less than forty years old. The richly coloured carpet, imitation leather three-piece suite, plywood coffee table and plastic-fronted bar, complete with a small statue of a bull, the badly printed bullfighting poster and the ingrained smell of tobacco all belonged to another time.

She motioned him to sit down on the sofa as she slid into a chair which obviously she always sat in. Without looking, she reached for a packet of cigarettes and lighter on the side table and lit a cigarette, blowing the smoke in a stream towards the ceiling.

'So, Inspector, what do you need to know?' she asked, as Daykin took out his notebook and searched his pockets for a pen.

'I need to know,' said Daykin, finally finding a pen and scribbling on the corner of the notebook to make sure it was working, 'your cleaning routine.'

'Cleaning routine? What an odd question. We have to do the brass, clean the kitchen and the vestry, wipe the inside of the windows, change the altar cloths if the season has changed, polish all the woodwork and vacuum the carpets. After that, we make ourselves a cup of tea and then go home.'

'There are usually two of you?'

'That's right.'

'How long would all that normally take you?'

'We divide it, one does the brass, the vacuuming and changing the cloths, the other does the woodwork and cleans the kitchen, the vestry and the windows. That takes us about three hours.'

'So on Thursday it would take you double that?'

'Something like that, yes. I started at eleven o'clock and left just before five.'

'All I'm interested in is the woodwork and the vacuuming. Can you tell me what you do when you polish the wood.'

'You don't know how to polish wood?'

'I'm asking you how you polish the pews in the church.'

She glared at him, not sure if he was asking a serious question, or taking a rise out of her. She took a long pull at her cigarette and exhaled slowly, twin streams of smoke coming out of her nostrils, whilst she thought about it.

'I use a soft cloth,' she said eventually. 'I spray a little polish on it and I work methodically, starting at the top of the pew and going right down to the base. Then I polish the seat. I

169

work from the front of the church to the back. I start with the pews to the right of the nave, then the ones to the left and finishing with the ones in front of the lady altar.'

'So you would notice if there was anything on the floor?'

'Not necessarily, I concentrate on polishing the wood, I'm not spending a lot of time looking around me.'

'What about the vacuuming?'

He hadn't made any wise cracks about the polishing, so she decided that this question was serious, too.

'That's simple. I start at the altar and work my way to the back of the church.'

'Is there carpet between the pews?'

'Yes.'

'And you vacuum that?'

'Of course I do,' she said, loudly enough to tell him she was shocked that he had asked.

'And you would notice if there was anything on the floor between the pews?'

'Such as what?'

'Part of a shoelace.'

'Possibly not, if it was right under the back of the pews.'

'So it could have been there without you knowing?'

'No,' she said emphatically.

'But I thought you said—'

'I vacuum every square inch of those carpets; if anything like a broken shoelace had been caught in the vacuum cleaner I would have heard it.'

'Are you saying that the broken shoelace could not have been in the church when you cleaned it on Thursday?'

'It could not.'

'Would you mind if I took a short statement from you?'

'If you must,' she said, stubbing out the cigarette.

It was late morning when Daykin walked into the incident room. Jason Pullan, Trevor Crossley and Gillian McKenzie were writing notes and they had completed the house-to-house enquiries and were finishing off the paperwork. That took nearly as long as the footwork. Constable Harvey had borrowed Daykin's cardboard boxes as in- and out-trays to try to keep some sort of order in the piles of paperwork he now had to look through. Toby Peterson was on the telephone and Daykin sat down next to him and waited for him to finish the call.

'Let's see what we've got,' he said to everyone round the table.

'Constable McKenzie, what does the house-to-house tell us?'

'Negative, sir. The house-to-house, nobody saw anyone or anything suspicious. Not even Tony Hammond going into the church, let alone the killer.'

'DC Harvey, anything in the computer printouts?'

'Not yet, sir, but, as you can see, I'm only about a third of the way through them.'

Constable Harvey had never been known as a man who overworked himself.

'Toby, start with the post-mortem, has Martin Reynolds called?'

Toby Peterson smiled.

'He survived and only fainted once. As the pathologist told you at the church, you already know just about everything. Except, that is, time of death. He puts it at some time between eleven and twelve on Thursday night.'

'Have you heard anything from France?'

'Yes, Nice should be able to tell us something in a couple of hours, they've sent an officer to the hotel with the copy of the passport. Paris may be a few days.'

'There was something in the house-to-house, sir,' said McKenzie. 'Pete Tucker was coming out of The Feathers on the night Hammond was murdered and saw Malcolm Proctor making a call from the telephone box in the square at about eleven-fifteen.'

'How does he know it was Malcolm Proctor?'

'Red anorak, blue fisherman's hat.'

'It must have been too dark to see that.'

'As he left the phone box he stopped to light a cigarette. He seemed to have trouble with the matches and Tucker had a good long look at him by the time he got it lit.'

Daykin looked round the table.

'I have something to tell you,' he said. 'Forensics found a broken shoelace in the church. The church was cleaned on Thursday, which means that the shoelace appeared between five and eleven o'clock on Thursday evening, it may have come from the shoes worn by the killer. So what does that tell us?'

There was a silence round the table while everyone thought. Except Terry Harvey, who had lost interest.

'The shoelace was brown, so it's likely that the shoes were as well. They must be lace-up shoes, probably worn by a man and not a woman. Anything else?' said Daykin.

'Do we know the make or age of the lace?' asked Toby Peterson.

'Good point, make a note to ask the SOCO, will you?'

'All right, people, let's make this afternoon the end of the paperwork to date, so we can all start on more interesting things tomorrow. Terry, do you mind if I take a look through the paperwork you've already seen?'

Harvey, who would have been happier for Daykin to look

through the papers he had not yet seen, nodded and pushed the cardboard box across the table.

The afternoon passed in almost total silence, interrupted only by the occasional telephone call or someone making a cup of tea. At six Daykin called a halt and they all left for the evening.

Before Daykin went into the house he took the dog for a long walk. When he got home he looked in the larder and the fridge to see what he had to eat. He felt in the mood to cook so he grilled a steak and made a green pepper sauce, sitting down to eat both with mange-touts and oven-roasted cour-gettes with couscous boiled in vegetable stock. After washing up he took the dog for another shorter walk, checked that the television had, as usual, nothing he wanted to watch and went to bed early.

When he woke with a start the first thing he did was to check the bedside clock. It was 3.22 a.m. and what in his sleep had been troubling him had crystallized in his mind. In a village as small as Camleigh, where everyone sees every-thing, two people, one following the other, would not have been missed. Tony Hammond was not seen because he didn't want to be, which meant that the killer had told him to get to the church for a secret meeting that nobody should know about. And that meant that when he arrived, some time between eleven o'clock and midnight, the killer was waiting for him.

The killer, who wore brown shoes, had enough of a hold over Tony Hammond to make him go to a meeting in the church just before midnight. Who fitted that profile?

CHAPTER TWENTY-EIGHT

'Is now a good time to talk to Malcolm Proctor?' said Toby Peterson.

'Sounds good to me. I need to find out why people think he had something to do with these deaths.'

By the time Daykin's fourth knock on the door went unanswered, although they could hear a dog barking somewhere at the back of the house, they knew that Malcolm Proctor was out. They tried The Feathers, but there was no sign of him. They walked up and down the High Street and called the station to see if anyone had seen him, but Malcolm Proctor had disappeared. Daykin put out a call for anyone who saw Proctor to contact him. They decided that that was all they could do, for now.

'Let's check the telephone box,' said Daykin.

They walked across the square to where the old red telephone box stood. It was not used much now that most people had mobile telephones and it showed signs of neglect. Three panels of glass were missing, the paintwork was beginning to peel away from the layers of rust and the graffiti on the inside of the box looked as if it had been there for some time.

'Does Malcolm Proctor have a mobile telephone?' asked

Daykin, as he took out his notebook and wrote down the telephone number.

'I don't know, sir, but I would think so.'

'Then why,' said Daykin, putting the notebook back in his pocket, 'would he make a call from a public telephone box at eleven-fifteen at night?'

'Perhaps he'd forgotten his mobile, or it had run out of credit.'

'Possibly. Let's see if we can find the number he called.' Daykin picked up the phone and dialled the operator.

This is Inspector Daykin, I'd like to check a number that was dialled by someone from this box at eleven-fifteen on Thursday night.'

'You'll have to go through the police liaison officer.'

'Who?'

'The police liaison officer.'

'Can't you tell me?'

'I don't know you from Adam. For all I know you are a jealous husband trying to find out who his wife called, and that's private. The police liaison officer will check out you're who you say you are and give you the information.'

'Can I have the number?'

When it was given to him, Daykin wrote it in his notebook, then dialled it. He explained what he needed, was asked a few questions that he knew would be checked through the police station and was given a password, so that when she called back the police liaison officer could make sure that she was talking to him. Daykin and Peterson hung around by the telephone box, Daykin wishing he had the sense to give her his mobile number, for ten minutes until the telephone rang. Daykin picked it up and gave the password. He was given the information.

'Can you repeat the address?' he asked.

It was repeated.

'Are you sure?'

She was sure.

'Was the telephone answered?'

It was, and there was a short conversation lasting thirty seconds.

Daykin thanked the police liaison officer and put the telephone down.

'Who did he call?' asked Toby Peterson.

'He called his home number,' said Daykin.

'Why?' asked Peterson.

'I don't know; the important question is who answered the telephone if he was here?'

Toby Peterson didn't answer. There wasn't an easy answer.

'Let's go back to the station,' said Daykin.

On the way Daykin's mobile phone rang and he scrambled through his pockets to find it.

'Tom?' said a voice as he put it to his ear, 'it's Andy. I've finished the accounts you gave me.'

'Anything interesting?'

'Only that his financial problems got worse last year.'

'How so?'

'It's those bloody visits to France. In the previous twelve months he made five, last year it was seven.'

'Still working at a loss?'

'Larger than the year before. If the furniture he brought back was sold at a fifteen per cent profit, he could have made a reasonable amount of money. As it was, it looks as if he was trying to give it away at any price he could get for it.'

'You're the accountant, what's the answer?'

'I haven't got one, just a second question.'

'Which is?'

'With regular losses like this, why did he keep his business going?'

'Or how.'

'That's easy. Regular injections of money.'

'Where from?'

'I don't know, the bank statements say they were cash.'

'Thanks, Andy.'

'Pleasure, I'll send you my bill. Give me a call if you want a beer some time.'

When they arrived at the station, the incident room had gone quiet. The house-to-house enquiries had been completed and reports had been written and reviewed. The police intelligence reports and computer printouts had been read and filed. The SOCO's report and post-mortem findings were finished and had been read. Now what was needed was a major lead.

Daykin looked at the three uniformed officers and the CID officers who were sitting round the table.

'From now until you go off-duty, I want you all to search for Malcolm Proctor. If you find him, arrest him on suspicion of murder. When you bring him back, telephone me if I'm not here. Any questions?'

Five heads shook from side to side.

'This is urgent,' said Daykin and there was the sound of chair legs scraping on the floor as the officers got up to leave.

Toby Peterson heard the fax machine start up and walked over to it.

'Looks like you have your replies from France,' he said, carrying the papers to where Daykin was standing. Daykin took them and translated aloud into English as he read them. He started with the shorter one.

'Inspector Labrun in Cannes confirms that Yvette Benastre positively identified the man in the passport photograph as Jonathan Lister.'

'What does that tell us?' asked Toby Peterson.

'That Michael Hilliam drove his dark blue Transit van to Kent, changed vans and his identity and drove the white Mercedes Sprinter to Paris, where he left it and went off to enjoy himself gambling in the South of France.'

'Why?'

'I'm hoping that the other fax will tell us that.' said Daykin, turning the pages.

'Whenever he arrived in Paris,' he began, frowning at the occasional word of Parisian slang, 'Hilliam would leave the van in the Porte de Vanves district which is the antique and flea market centre. He had an arrangement with one of the dealers who would, while he was away in the South of France, load the van up with antiques. When Hilliam returned, he would pay the dealer and drive the van back to England. The dealer thought Hilliam, or Lister as he knew him, was a bit lazy, but he paid good money and in cash when he collected the van. There is a statement here from the dealer and one from Sergent Dupont.'

'Do you see it all now?' asked Toby Peterson.

'Do I know why Michael Hilliam went to France? Yes. Do I know why he was killed? I'm pretty certain I do. Do I know who killed him? I thought I did, now I'm not so sure.'

'What now, sir?' asked Peterson.

Daykin looked at his watch.

'It's getting late and I'd like to get an early start in the morning. Why don't you go home now and I'll meet you in my office at seven thirty. The morning should start off with a bang.'

Toby Peterson watched Daykin walk out, but he didn't make any move himself. If only they knew it at this police station, he dreaded going home. They all joked about conversations over the dinner table, if only they knew what a selfish, overbearing bully his father was.

In his middle teens Toby Peterson had a clear vision of what he wanted to do with his life. He would be a historian, hopefully a military historian. He would write articles and books give lectures and lead the life of an academic. But his father was determined that at least one of his sons would follow him into the police force. Toby's elder brother had escaped while he still could, selecting a university as far away from North Yorkshire as possible, then interviewing for a job with a venture capital bank in London even before he took his finals.

So Toby it was who had to join the police force. Any argument was dealt with by harsh words or, on occasions, the threat of violence from his father. The fear of his father, instilled into him with a walking stick at a very young age, had never really left him.

When he went home there would be no civilized dinner table conversations, just a long and searching interrogation into his working day.

But they didn't need to know that at this station. Let them have their fantasies. Sadly he put his notebook away. He had better get home before too long. The old man might be in a better mood tonight. Better not risk antagonizing him by being late.

There was not a lot of warmth in the Peterson household, the money that had bought the great gothic building, the size of a small hotel, was the main reason for that.

Grandfather Peterson had been a good businessman and

had built a large engineering company from nothing, running it until a conglomerate from Sheffied bought it for far more than he thought it was worth. The talents that had made him so good at his job, being dour, humourless, bigoted and domineering, he had passed on to his eldest son.

If it was a bad evening it would follow the same course. As Toby went through the front door, Mahler would be playing on the stereo. That meant that his father was home. He would follow the melancholic sound of the music and find his father in the living room, pouring two fingers of brandy into a cut glass tumbler and topping it with a splash of soda from the mesh covered siphon. He would be invited to pour his own drink. This was not a warm invitation, it was a sign that his father wanted to lecture him.

He would be asked about his day, every detail of it. He would be told not to get too close to his superiors, because one day he would outrank them. Not to get too comfortable at his present station, because one day soon he would be moving on.

He would repeat his dismay that his son had wasted time after university backpacking through Thailand, Indonesia, Vietnam and India. How the university years had been frittered away on rowing, drinking and spending his time with people who would never be useful to him in later life.

The lecture would last through one, and if it started early, two drinks and on a bad night through the meal and, as they moved back to the living-room, coffee. The elder Peterson saw his younger son as an extension of his own massive ambition. He would rise to the same, or perhaps better, rank than he enjoyed. It would be a dynasty and if the boy's – for he still thought of him as a boy – resolve waivered then these regular talks would firm it up.

He enjoyed these evenings and never gave a thought to how his son might feel.

When Toby Peterson got home Mahler was on the stereo and his father was in the armchair.

'Pour yourself a drink, Toby,' he said, picking up the evening paper. It was not a good sign.

While he poured himself three fingers of Scotch his father opened the paper and started to read. When he spoke to his son he didn't lower it, he talked through it.

'I had a call from your Superintendent Jarvis today.'

'Superintendent Jarvis?'

'You don't have to repeat everything I say. Yes, you mark my words, he's a man who is going places. You could do a lot worse than watch how he works if you want rapid promotion. Anyway, he has decided to take that inspector – Daykin is it – off the case.'

Toby Peterson used the silver tongs to add two cubes of ice to his drink.

'That would be a mistake,' he said, with enough force to make his father put the paper down.

'I don't think it's for you to question the decisions of a man who outranks you by a long way.'

'Tom Daykin is the best copper I've worked with. He's intelligent and hard working, but it's not just that, he has a feel for a case. If he's replaced now it would do a lot of harm because I know he's close. Very close.'

Assistant Chief Constable Peterson took his time reaching for his drink from the side table and taking a good long swallow.

'I can see you feel strongly about it.' he said eventually. 'I'll have a word with Mark Jarvis. Make sure you tell that inspector that he owes you a large favour.'

'I probably will,' said Toby Peterson, who had no intention of saying anything to Daykin. In the meantime his father would not let him forget the favour his son owed to him.

There was more pleasure in the evening Mark Jarvis and Paula Sykes shared. This time Jarvis read the signs well. He had packed an overnight bag and told his wife that he had to attend an evening meeting at headquarters in Northallerton that wouldn't finish until late, so he would stay overnight.

After the theatre they had walked to a small Italian restaurant where they both ate their meals a little too quickly before driving back to Paula Sykes's house. After thirty minutes of rising passion on her living-room sofa a flirtation turned into an affair and they went to bed.

CHAPTER TWENTY-NINE

Toby Peterson hadn't lost any sleep over Daykin's last remark about the morning starting with a bang, although it had puzzled him. When he walked into the inspector's office just before half past seven, he saw what Daykin had meant.

Lying across the desk was a bright yellow metal object, about three feet long and shaped like a very large bullet. It had metal handles welded to both sides. Toby Peterson recognized it immediately. It was a battering ram, used to force entry to property. A skilful operator could open a locked steel door in seconds.

'I've kicked a few doors in in my time and, believe me, it's not as easy as they make it appear in the films. If you've got the equipment, you might as well use it, so I've drawn this from stores.'

'Whose door is going in?' asked Peterson, who could think of several candidates.

'Malcolm Proctor's.'

'Have you got a warrant to do this?'

'I don't need one. He's a suspect. When I came in this morning, I looked at the intelligence from the enquiries made last night and no one has seen him. That means he's probably

183

hiding at his home. We heard the dog barking when we called there. I don't think he doted on it, but I can't see him leaving the village and abandoning it. So, we have reasonable suspicion that a suspect is in the property, we have the right to enter without a warrant.'

Toby Peterson didn't like the 'we' in the last sentence, but he'd never seen a ram used before, so he just nodded.

When they got out of the vehicle outside Malcolm Proctor's house, Toby Peterson carefully opened the rickety garden gate and Daykin walked down the short path, carrying the battering ram in one hand as casually as if it was made of polystyrene. He knocked once on the door as if he didn't expect an answer, then measured the ram against the door lock, swung it back in an underarm arc and brought it crashing against the door. There was a simultaneous crash of metal against wood and a sharp crack as the door round the lock splintered into twenty pieces which flew in different directions. The door swung back so violently that it rebounded off the interior wall and arced back towards them again. It would have closed itself if the lock, which was now hanging off the door by a single splinter of wood, had still been working. Instead it hit the doorjamb and the door then moved slowly away from them again, as if unsure what to do. The shattered lock fell on to the hall carpet with a dull thud.

Inside the house the dog started barking again, but the rest was silence. Daykin put the battering ram down on the hall floor.

'Malcolm Proctor!' he called through the open door.

The dog's barking increased, then died away. Daykin and Peterson could now hear something else, a very soft creaking sound, like the noises of an old sailing ship riding at anchor.

It did not take them long to find Malcolm Proctor, or identify the creaking noise. Three feet into the hallway two steps climbed to the left to a small half landing before the stairway turned to the right to run up to the first floor. On that floor and over the half landing was a short railing. A rope had been tied to the railing. At the bottom of the rope, his neck in a noose and his feet dangling lifelessly eighteen inches from the floor, was Malcolm Proctor. As the body turned slowly, the rope creaked against the wood of the railings.

Standing behind Daykin, Toby Peterson gave a short involuntary shudder.

'I'd better cut him down,' he said.

'No, just call the SOCO and Forensics,' said Daykin, looking sadly at the bulging eyes and swollen tongue of the distorted face. 'They'll want to see the body *in situ*. We only cut him down if there is a chance of reviving him.'

While they waited for the scientists to arrive they made a search of the house, but found nothing. The dog had been locked in a small larder cupboard of the kitchen. Daykin let it out into the overgrown back garden. They were just finishing the search when there was a knock on the front door, which they had wedged shut with a chair to stop the prying eyes of the neighbours. Daykin opened the door and let the pathologist in.

'Long time since I've seen a suicide by hanging, it seems to have gone out of fashion,' said Dr Caisley, casting a professional eye over the body.

'I'll do what I can for now, but I won't be able to make my preliminary examination until he's cut down and I suppose that can't be done until the photographer has finished with him.'

He didn't have to wait long. The Crime Scene Investigation

team arrived within ten minutes and the hallway was soon full of men in white plastic suits and the irregular series of flashes, like a lightning storm, of the photographs being taken.

'This is becoming a weekly event, Tom. The mortuary say that they were having a quiet time until you started this investigation,' said the CSI officer after they had cut the body down and they both stood watching the pathologist as he examined it in the hallway.

'It's not what the mortuary staff say that bothers me, it's what Jarvis will make of it.'

'Good point,' said Phil Carter. One of his white-suited team walked past him. 'Is Garvey in the van?' he asked.

'Yes, Sarge.'

'Tell him to put the kettle on for a cup of tea.'

'Tell him to make one for me, I'm finished here,' said Dominic Caisley. 'OK, boys!' he called to two slim middle-aged men in black suits who had silently entered the house carrying a folding trolley fifteen minutes earlier. They had seated themselves in the dining-room and sat there patiently, talking to no one, not even each other. They were the pathologist's assistants and their job was to take the body to the mortuary. They worked unhurriedly, but with surprising speed as they laid a dark green heavy plastic bag beside the body, gently lifted it into the bag and zipped it up. One of them racked the trolley and they lifted the bag on to it, strapping it on and rolling it through the front door.

'I need a favour,' said Daykin to the pathologist, as they watched the body wheeled out of sight.

'You've been such a regular customer, how could I refuse?' replied Dr Caisley, smiling up at Daykin over his gold half-moon glasses.

'I'd like you to perform the post-mortem in a hurry and I'd like to be there.'

Dominic Caisley pursed his lips.

'I'll need to make a couple of calls to book the autopsy room and get my assistants to prepare the body.'

'How long do you think?'

'I really can't say, but I've got your mobile number, I'll call you as soon as I can organize everything.'

He followed his assistants up the short front path, stopping at the CSI van for his cup of tea while they drove away in an estate car with darkened windows.

'Anything more we can do here, sir?' asked Toby Peterson over Daykin's shoulder.

'No, let's go back to the station and start the paperwork again.'

The level of activity in the incident room had gone back up to frantic. Paperwork was being processed, two new officers had been drafted in and the inevitable house-to-house enquiries had begun. Daykin sat in what was now his usual seat and began to complete the forms that started all major investigations. He did not get far.

'This is becoming an epidemic, Daykin!' said Jarvis's voice from the door.

Daykin looked up. 'Your office, sir?' he asked.

'Immediately,' replied Jarvis and was gone.

'Keep them busy, Toby,' said Daykin. shuffling his papers into a neat pile and placing them with exaggerated care on the table.

He knocked on Superintendent Jarvis's office door loudly, more loudly than he intended.

'Come,' said Jarvis's voice.

'Sit down, Daykin,' he began, pointing to one of the two

chairs on the other side of the desk.

But Daykin didn't sit down. Instead he started pacing backwards and forwards across the room.

'Do you think I'm killing these people off?' he shouted. 'Using a knife and a rope to make work for myself! Or do you think I could have done anything to stop any of these murders! Tell me if something strikes you!'

'Calm down, Inspector,' Jarvis found himself saying, waving his hands up and down in what passed for a calming motion. 'The chief constable—'

'Stuff the chief constable! I've got bodies piling up and the only help I get from you is to tell me the chief constable won't be pleased! Now, I've got an investigation that's ongoing, so I'll make my way back to the incident room. Tell the chief constable we're doing our best and if he wants to roll up his sleeves and come and give us a hand, he'll be more than welcome!'

He stormed out of the office, making sure he slammed the door behind him. It hadn't done his promotion prospects any good, but it made him feel a whole lot better.

'The pathologist's been on the telephone, sir,' said Toby Peterson as Daykin walked back into the incident room, 'he says he can do the post-mortem in an hour.'

'Coming?'

'I've a lot to do, sir,' said Peterson lamely.

'Don't worry, I think I can just about manage on my own. Car keys?'

Toby Peterson slid them across the table.

The post-mortem was at Richmond Hospital and by the time the traffic had delayed him, Daykin walked into the building with five minutes to spare.

'Inspector,' said Dr Caisley, now dressed in a dark green

operating gown and a long rubber apron. He was standing at the door of the autopsy room, just about to push it open. 'After all the fuss, I was afraid you'd found something more important to do.'

'Wouldn't have missed it for the world,' said Daykin, following him through the door.

The autopsy room was about twenty feet square and windowless. The walls were white-tiled, the floor terrazzo. It was brightly lit, and the stainless steel table in the centre was bathed in a pool of brighter light from a bank of spotlights. The only sound was the gentle gurgle of water as it sluiced from the top of the table to the bottom, running around the body of Malcolm Proctor which now lay on it.

At the other side of the table, also now in green operating gowns and long rubber aprons, were the two men Daykin had seen earlier, at the house. They stood at the far side of another trolley, this one stainless steel and holding the surgical instruments the pathologist would use. They stared identical baleful stares at Daykin as he walked in.

'The inspector is in a hurry, so let's begin,' said Dominic Caisley, turning on a microphone and looking at the notes of height, age, weight and physical description the assistants had made since bringing the body to the mortuary.

'No Detective Reynolds today?' asked the pathologist casually.

'Not his favourite pasttime.'

'Male, one point seven metres exactly, approximately forty years old, scars to the left forehead and right knee. Well-nourished without obvious signs of disease,' began the pathologist, his mouth six inches from the microphone. 'Let's start by taking a look at the brain.'

One of the assistants passed him a small circular saw.

'I'm taking the top of the skull off,' said Dr Caisley, testing the saw by pressing the on switch several times, 'not queasy are we, Inspector?'

'I'll survive.'

The post-mortem was routine, until the pathologist's examination reached the stomach.

'That's odd,' he said, almost to himself.

Daykin did not say anything, but coughed softly to remind Dr Caisely that he was there.

'This man really meant to kill himself,' said the doctor. 'There appears to be a large amount of barbiturates in the stomach.'

'Odd?' prompted Daykin.

'People react differently to massive doses of barbiturates; he must have been still awake when he put the rope round his neck, but I would have expected him to be comatose.'

'Could the barbiturates have killed him on their own?'

'Impossible to say until I've analysed the stomach contents and done the bloodwork, but I would doubt it.'

The pathologist continued his work until he concluded, 'Death by asphyxiation as the result of a ligature round the neck, probably self-administered.'

'He hanged himself?' asked Daykin.

'Precisely.'

Daykin left Dr Caisley to write his report and drove to the Crime Scene Investigation office.

'Don't tell me, you want a full report,' said Sergeant Carter as Daykin walked through the door.

'Something like that.'

'Too early, but I'll tell you what I know.'

'Go on.'

'There's nothing much to talk about in the house. I've sent

off some fingerprints for identification, but I'm pretty certain that they will prove to be poor old Malcolm's. No mysterious footprints in the flowerbeds and the rope he used to top himself was cut from a length in the outhouse that looks as if it had been there for years. All the signs are that he tied it to the first-floor railing, climbed to about halfway up the stairs, put the noose round his neck and jumped.'

'But?'

'No suicide note. Oh, I know not every suicide leaves one, but someone who goes to these lengths usually does.'

'Anything else?'

'Nothing to tell you yet. We've sent the usual samples off for forensics but, as I say, there's nothing in the house to make me think that this was anything but a suicide.'

'Why would he kill himself?'

'No note, so I don't know.'

'Sorry I asked.'

CHAPTER THIRTY

SENIOR officers like Mark Jarvis bear grudges. They have a way of getting back at you. Jarvis would be upset by Daykin's outburst in his office and there would be a payback, Daykin was waiting for it. What he got was something he didn't expect.

'Superintendent Jarvis's office, do not pass go, do not collect two hundred pounds,' said the custody sergeant as Daykin walked into the station.

'Who says?'

'He did. Said you had to report to his office as soon as you got in.'

'I've been expecting it.'

'Then you better get it over with,' said the sergeant, who began to hum the Dead March as Daykin walked down the corridor. If this was the day for paybacks, Daykin decided that Sergeant Pullan would be next.

He knocked on the superintendent's door, a little softer this time.

'Come,' shouted Jarvis, confident as ever.

'Tom,' he said as Daykin walked in. 'Sit you down.'

Cautiously, Daykin took a seat.

'Well,' began Superintendent Jarvis expansively, 'a job well done.'

Daykin looked at him quizzically, but said nothing. When Mark Jarvis was in this sort of mood, it was best just to let him have his say.

'I've spoken to the people upstairs and they agree that it has all sorted itself out quite nicely.'

He waited for Daykin to ask him how, but as there was only silence, he continued.

'Obviously, Malcolm Proctor killed Michael Hilliam, then Tony Hammond, then unable to bear the burden of his guilt, he took his own life. Case closed.'

'Motive?' asked Daykin.

'I don't know, but I'm confident you'll find one. Perhaps he wanted to be churchwarden and killed everyone in his way.'

'Not the best motive for murder, sir.'

'There have been worse. You seem to have missed the religious zealot angle; stigmata. Malcolm Proctor's waters ran very deep. Anyway, everyone from me upwards agrees that is the scenario, so just tie up the loose ends, will you? I've notified the Portakabin people that they can pick it up within the next three days.'

'A bit sudden isn't, sir?'

'Not at all. The last thing either you or I want is three unsolved deaths ongoing with open files gathering dust. Far better to close it off and move on, don't you see?'

'And you think that's what happened?' said Daykin.

'I do. Case closed, Inspector,' replied Mark Jarvis firmly. 'Wrap it up.'

Daykin saw that sitting there and arguing would only

mean that Jarvis would give him a direct order to close the case. For all he knew Jarvis could be right, but it was his investigation and he didn't want to be ordered to end it.

'I'll start putting things in motion, sir,' he lied, as he got up to go.

'Inspector,' said Jarvis as he got to the door, 'this will look good on my record and especially on yours.'

'Toby,' said Daykin as he walked into the incident room, 'let's have a chat.'

He took Peterson to the corner of the room furthest from the others.

'Jarvis has given us three days to close this investigation.'

'But we've hardly started!' protested Toby Peterson.

'He's got it into his head that Proctor killed both Hilliam and Hammond, then committed suicide. And I think that's what he's told the chief constable.'

'Do you want me to have a word with my father?'

'No, that's the last thing I want you to do. I don't want anything said to him, understand?'

'Yes, sir.'

'So we've got three days to close this case, but let's do it properly, let's solve it instead of going for the easy option.'

'Any suggestions, sir?'

'Let's start with Malcolm Proctor. If we can find out why he committed suicide, the rest will fall into place. Concentrate on that. I'll try to keep the two extra officers we've got. You and I will read every scrap of paperwork between us and just hope to God something comes out of the woodwork.'

As they started the paperwork Chief Inspector Sykes walked through the door and up to the table where Daykin was sitting.

'I've come to offer the olive branch, Inspector Daykin,' she said.

'How so, ma'am?' asked Daykin, genuinely surprised.

'You and I have had our differences, but Superintendent Jarvis tells me you have a solution to this case and you're now closing it.'

'I didn't know you continued to be interested in this investigation, ma'am.'

'To tell the truth,' said Paula Sykes smugly, 'I was the one who suggested to Superintendent Jarvis that Malcolm Proctor was a double murderer who committed suicide.'

'Why would Malcolm Proctor commit suicide?'

'The net's closing after two murders. The pending paedophile investigations. He had a lot of reasons. Anyway, I'm glad it's all sorted out and we can all get on with other things.'

She nodded curtly to Peterson and walked out.

'Everything seems to have turned out for the best,' said Toby Peterson sarcastically.

'Whether it's over or not,' said Daykin, 'there's paperwork to do.'

'There's always paperwork to do,' said Peterson, turning back to the untidy piles on the table in front of him.

While Toby Peterson was cursing his job, Daykin took a break and went back to his office.

In many ways the community of North Yorkshire is a small one and that was sometimes useful. He had a second cousin who worked in the force's Human Resources Office. He telephoned her and told her he needed details from some files. He wanted details from the personnel files of every officer who was involved in the case, including Jarvis and

Sykes. The details were given without question, it was family.

'See if you can dig up some background,' he said, 'anything outside the file you can find out.'

CHAPTER THIRTY-ONE

DAYKIN sat at his desk and thought for a long time before reaching for the directory in a rack behind his desk. He looked up the section for the Crown Prosecution Service. He found the department that was located in Birmingham and dialled the number.

'David Moore, please.'

David Moore was an old friend. They had played rugby and got drunk together more times than he could remember in the far-off days of their youth.

'David Moore,' said a once familiar voice.

'David, Tom Daykin. How are you?'

'Tom, you're not local, are you?'

'No, still in North Yorkshire.'

'Pity, it's getting near opening time.'

'I need a large favour, Dave.'

'Try me.'

'There was a road traffic accident about two years ago somewhere on the outskirts of Birmingham, it may have involved a death. The case was stopped before it got to court. I need some details from the file.'

'You haven't given me much to go on, do you know

anything else?'

'The suspect was Tony Hammond, but he probably went by a different name then.'

'Ten years ago I'd have said impossible to trace, but these days of computers I may just be able to pull the file.'

'Thanks, Dave,' said Daykin. He gave David Moore his mobile telephone number and hung up. He went back to the incident room to look through the papers. He couldn't concentrate and spent most of the time drumming his fingers on the table or getting up to pace around the room. Just over two hours later his telephone rang.

'Anything, Dave?'

'You don't make life easy,' said David Moore. 'That file wasn't too difficult to trace, there aren't many deaths by dangerous driving files, but there was a stop order on it.'

'Stop order?'

'The file becomes restricted, only people with the proper authority can view it.'

'So you can't tell me anything about it?'

'I asked someone to do me a favour. She has the authority, she looked at the file and gave me the details.'

'What do you have?'

'Not a lot. The man you call Tony Hammond was going by the name of Paul Hawkins, but that wasn't his real name either. He was driving through Edgbaston early one evening when he knocked someone down and killed her. He had been drinking all afternoon and gave a positive breath test. About two hours after he was charged, the heavy mob arrived from Scotland Yard with the paperwork to take him away with them. Three days later the Crown Prosecution Service in Birmingham received an authority from the Home Office to stop proceedings and put the file in the restricted category.

"In the interests of the State", they said.'

'Who died?'

'I can't tell you, just a pedestrian.'

'Thanks, Dave, I owe you one.'

'Next time you're in Birmingham, you're buying.'

On the drive home Daykin decided that he was hungry, but he didn't feel like cooking. He stopped at the Chinese take-away and took a meal home with him.

He was sitting down at the kitchen table when he looked at the morning's paper. He ordered *The Times* from the local newsagents and it was not usually delivered until he had left for work. In the evenings he was too tired to read it and for months he had been thinking about cancelling it. He had picked it off the hall mat with the morning's post when he came in and laid it carelessly on the table. It had fallen open at the business section, which he didn't usually read. A small headline near the foot of the page caught his eye. Some middle man in the city had made an obscene amount of money putting a buyer and seller together and claiming his commission. There was a photograph of him, a large cigar clamped between his teeth.

'I only took advantage of the opportunity offered to me,' he was quoted as saying.

Daykin looked at the quote, the forkful of chow mein halfway to his mouth.

'I have been so stupid,' he said softly to himself, 'why didn't I see that earlier?'

CHAPTER THIRTY-TWO

SOMETIMES one enormous piece of luck can move a case forward more than weeks of patient sifting through evidence. Daykin needed some luck and as he sat at his desk the following morning, trying to work out how to approach the problem, he got it. The telephone rang.

'That posh-sounding policeman from London,' said Mavis, 'line two.'

'Inspector Daykin? Christopher Bennett. I've a bit of interesting information for you.'

'What sort of information?'

Bennett, who was not used to be interrupted, ignored him.

'My people went to Tony Hammond's house yesterday to tidy up. We don't want anything' – he searched for the word – 'embarrassing.'

'They wouldn't find much, we searched the place. I didn't know they were coming.'

'They removed certain things that a cursory search wouldn't show. As far as not knowing they were coming, even if you had a written invitation, you wouldn't know they were there, or had been.

'One of the items they removed,' he continued, 'was a

CCTV camera which sends signals to a video recorder at. . . . Well, you don't need to know where the video recorder is.'

'If there was a camera we'd have found it, we're not that stupid.'

'You searched the house, the camera was mounted in a tree in the copse next to the garden. It was trained on Tony Hammond's front door, so we could see who came and went. One of my men looked through the last few night's videos yesterday and he saw something that may well interest you. I'm sending the tape to you by courier. Look at it starting about five minutes before midnight.'

Daykin didn't know what to say.

'Thanks,' he said eventually.

'Not at all, Inspector. Despite appearances, we're all in the same boat, sometimes even rowing in the same direction.'

It could not have been more than ten minutes later that Sergeant Pullan on the front desk called.

'Messenger with a parcel here for you, Tom. I've tried to sign for it, but he insists he wants to hand it to you and to no one else.'

'I know what it is. I'll come out and sign for it, Harry.'

The courier wanted to see Daykin's warrant card and examined his signature, comparing it to the one on the card, before handing over the padded envelope.

'Be careful how you open that, it could be a bomb,' said the sergeant.

He and Daykin smiled at each other, although the joke was too obvious to be funny.

On his way back to his office Daykin gently felt the package. There was definitely a video cassette inside it.

'Birthday present, sir?' asked Toby Peterson who had just arrived and hurried down the corridor to catch up to Daykin.

They had reached Daykin's office door.

'Come in and sit down, Toby, I've something to say to you.'

As they got inside the office Daykin made sure that the door was shut.

'I want you to go through the motions of wrapping this case up today,' he began. 'Finish off reading the paperwork, then start packing it into boxes. Make sure that the uniforms have finished their reports, then reassign them to other cases. Same with Harvey and Reynolds. Get as much furniture as possible out of the Portakabin, because I think that Jarvis will have arranged for it to be collected tomorrow. If Jarvis or Sykes ask, we are closing the investigation, the conclusion is that Proctor murdered Hilliam and Hammond, then committed suicide.'

'What will you be doing?'

'I think that there may be another solution, but I'm not sure that I'm right. If I'm wrong, there's going to be a volcanic eruption and I can't ask you to stand in the way of the lava flow.'

Peterson, the Assisant Chief Constable, had a reputation for determination and now Daykin saw that some of it had rubbed off on his son.

'This is not your investigation, sir. It's ours. If we're reaching the end of it. I want to be there. You owe it to me not to exclude me. If there's going to be a firing squad to face. I can face it just as well as you can.'

'So be it,' said Daykin, with what Toby Peterson thought might be slight smile, 'let's take a look at this video.'

It was not the clearest of pictures, more like the hazy monochrome of early television than the bright, crisp colours of a modern screen. But it was taken at night through a night vision lens. The buildings and any movement could be seen and the pictures were just clear enough to identify figures and vehicles. It was just a strain on the eyes and the action round Tony Hammond's house at midnight wasn't exactly Charing Cross Station. They watched a completely still screen, their eyes becoming more and more strained until the small white figures at the top left of the screen showed that the time read 23.58 p.m.

'It can't be,' said Toby Peterson softly.

'I think it is,' replied Daykin. 'It fits what I was thinking.'

He rewound the tape for four minutes and they watched it again.

'What now, sir?' said Toby Peterson, thinking that he seemed to be using that phrase a lot lately.

'I need to go to see a magistrate. I should do that on my own, or it will look like the Star Chamber. You start putting the paperwork away; it's more important than ever that you do that now.'

'And after the magistrate?'

'There's a search. If we find what I think we will, then there's an arrest. You should be part of both.'

Daykin took the tape out of the machine and put it back into the padded bag.

'Do you want me to put that somewhere safe?' asked Toby Peterson.

'No. I think I may need it.'

The only person who can issue a search warrant is a magistrate. Daykin looked at his watch as he walked back to his office. It would take him about two hours to complete the paperwork that would satisfy the magistrate that he had enough grounds to search a house. He telephoned the court. Would they have a magistrate available at noon? They would. He took a form from his desk drawer and began to write.

Exactly two hours later he checked the form and the other documents for the last time, put them carefully into his brief-case and got up to leave. He did not tell anyone where he was going. The less his superiors knew, the better.

It was not a long journey from the police station to the court, but it was raining, so he took the car and parked it under the lean-to roof at the side of the tiny car-park beside the building.

The courthouse was small, not like the great concrete and glass tower blocks in the cities, but it was large enough for its community. Like the people who worked in it, it was solid and dependable. Built of large blocks of Dales stone in an age long before computers, faxes or even telephones, it had done little to adapt to modern life. In winter the old-fashioned green radiators, fed by a coal-fuelled boiler, gurgled and hissed alarmingly, but seemed to throw out enough heat to warm the building. In summer people who had never heard of air conditioning opened the windows when it was warm.

Daykin climbed the well-trodden steps to the front door, over which a royal coat of arms carved in stone had suffered the abrasion of wind and rain for enough years to be worn away in patches. He opened the door and was faced with a dark oak counter, topped by vertical glass screens, like a bank, behind which the five or six court staff worked at their desks. A tiny middle-aged woman saw him and walked to the counter. Doris Shaw, the Assistant Chief Clerk.

'Tom Daykin, what brings you here?' she asks.

'I've got a warrant to swear, Doris.'

'Where's your dog?' she asked, getting up on her toes and leaning to one side to look behind him.

'He's in the car.'

'Well, bring him in, I'm sure I have one of those chewable

bones in the cupboard in my office.'

'He'll be wet, Doris.'

'It doesn't matter, he can't stay in that car on his own, a dog his size.'

'On your head be it,' said Daykin, turning to walk back to the car.

When he brought the dog back on a short lead, Doris Shaw was holding the door in the counter open for him and he and the dog followed her to her office. The dog settled in the corner with a stick of rawhide and chewed contentedly, occasionally looking up to make sure no one was going to take this unexpected treat away from him. Doris looked down at it from her desk with a smile on her face. She genuinely liked Tom Daykin and had known him since they were at junior school together but, being single and childless, she looked on the dog as a child. In her heart of hearts, Doris Shaw preferred animals to humans every time.

'I'll tell the magistrate you're here,' she said.

'Inspector Daykin is here, sir,' she said into the telephone. She looked at Daykin. 'You can go up, he's in the chief clerk's office.'

'Who have I got?' asked Daykin.

'Mr Cooper, the visiting district judge.'

Daykin groaned inwardly and couldn't help pulling a face. Some magistrates were better than others, some would sign a warrant as soon as they saw Daykin, simply because they trusted him. But Cooper was a very different proposition. For years he had been a solicitor and partner in one of the large criminal defence firms in Sheffield. In his late forties he decided that he wanted a quieter life as a professional magistrate, away from the grime and the crime of the industrial heartland. Now he had a pleasant and not too taxing life, spending half his time in Harrogate and Ripon and the rest visiting the small country courtrooms where, with a bit of luck, he could have finished his list by the early afternoon and go for a spot of fishing.

He had brought some of his former profession with him and was not known to be prosecution minded. 'Freedom Freddy' some of the officers called him, because of the number of people he let out on bail. This would not be easy.

'Don't you be disrespectful to my magistrate, Tom,' said Doris Shaw sternly, but there was a twinkle in her eye, 'and you know what he's like, you'd better not keep him waiting.'

Daykin slowly climbed the ornate oak staircase with its rich deep-blue carpet running down the centre of the steps. All the way up he was thinking about how he could persuade Freddy Cooper that he needed the warrant signing.

The chief clerk's office was just the sort of working environment that pompous middle management Victorian civil servants would design for themselves. A large leather-topped desk dominated the centre of the room, placed in front of a padded leather chair and on a Persian carpet that showed enough of the parquet floor between its edges and the scrolled skirting boards for the floor to be a nightmare to clean. There was a black-leaded fireplace with brass fire tools and fireguard, mullioned windows with window seats and tall wooden shutters, a moulded picture rail that ran round the whole of the room and from which oil painted landscapes, stained dark by the years, hung in gilded, pierced frames. Sitting at the desk, and staring at him, was Frederick Cooper JP.

The chief clerk, a tall, quietly spoken man sat at a small side desk working silently with his head bowed. He was relegated to this desk every time Cooper came to the courthouse. If it offended him he didn't show it.

'Sit down, Inspector,' said Freddy Cooper. 'Now, what's this all about?'

For the next twenty minutes Daykin, having passed the documents from his briefcase to Cooper, explained what he knew and what he suspected and why he wanted a warrant. For most of the time Cooper sat forward in his chair, reading the documents, not appearing to listen to a word Daykin was saying. Only when Daykin had finished that he put the papers on to the desktop and looked up.

'Is that it?' he asked.

Daykin nodded.

'On that pile of half-baked ideas and innuendo, you want me to give you a warrant to stamp with your size twelves all over someone else's property? Go squirrelling through their private possessions?'

He turned to the chief clerk.

'What do you think, Arnold?'

The chief clerk looked up from his work. Daykin could have sworn that he hadn't heard a word, but he had.

'I believe, sir, that the inspector has a sound application, based on deduction and logic. I can't see any real harm done by the issuing of a warrant in this case and, on the other hand, it may result in a proper conviction.'

'No, I don't think so,' replied Cooper. Both the chief clerk and Daykin knew that his opinion had only been asked for so Cooper could disagree with it. Cooper was a man who needed regular injections of steroids to his ego.

'I'm afraid it's just not good enough, Inspector, I can't grant a warrant on the evidence you have given me.' He paused, 'Is there anything else?'

'Just this, sir,' replied Daykin, leaning forward and taking the video tape from his briefcase, 'you might like to watch this before you make a final decision.'

There was a television and video unit in Court No 2, which was empty and Daykin and Frederick Cooper took the tape there. The chief clerk wasn't invited, which suited Daykin as, for now, the fewer people who knew about the contents of this tape, the better. Cooper insisted on watching the few minutes either side of midnight four times.

'Can you identify the people on that tape?' he said after the final viewing.

'I'm sure I can, sir.'

'Good enough for a court?'

'The quality is good enough for a facial mapping expert to make a positive identification from that tape.'

Cooper sat back in his chair and rubbed his eyes in tired resignation.

'You know the risks to your career if this goes wrong?'

'I do, sir,' said Daykin quietly.

'Then I'll grant the warrant and may God help you if you're not right.'

CHAPTER THIRTY-THREE

OUTSIDE the courthouse Daykin sat in his car and dialled the incident room on his mobile telephone. Toby Peterson answered.

'Toby, I've got the warrant, can I pick you up in five minutes?'

'Yes, sir.'

'Walk out of the car-park and along the road towards the High Street. I'll pick you up from there.'

'Why all the cloak and dagger, sir?'

'Better safe than sorry. See you in five minutes.'

Toby Peterson was twenty yards from the park gates at the end of the High Street when Daykin pulled his car to the kerb beside him, stopped and got out of the car.

'You drive, will you? I've a telephone call to make.'

'Where to, sir?'

'Camleigh.'

As Toby Peterson set off for the twenty-minute journey, Daykin pulled his diary out and looked up Andy Liddle's telephone number, before dialling it on his mobile telephone.

'Andy? Tom Daykin. Does your father still do some work

as a locksmith? Good, if he's in the shop, can you give me the number?'

He noted the number on a pad on his knee, thanked Andy Liddle, then redialled. 'Mr Liddle? It's Tom Daykin. Can you do a locksmith job for me this morning?'

'How long will it take?'

'About two hours.'

'When?'

'I can pick you up in ten minutes.'

'Who is going to pay me?'

'North Yorkshire Police.'

'I'll get Andy to mind the shop.'

Daykin made another call to make sure that the house would be empty.

Ten minutes later, as Toby Peterson stopped the car outside the shop, Mr Liddle was waiting for them in the shop doorway, an old army haversack on a strap over his right shoulder. He walked to the car and got into the back seat, throwing the haversack in before him. He saw Toby Peterson looking at it through the rear-view mirror.

'Tools of the trade,' he said.

On the way back to Shapford, Mr Liddle said, 'What's the address we are going to?'

'25 Rugby Drive,' replied Daykin.

'The new estate of houses on the edge of the town?'

'New' was not how Daykin would describe them, they were at least twenty-five years old, but he was not going to argue the point.

'That's it,' he said.

'Then it should be easy, I supplied the house locks to the builders. Unless they've been changed, it will be a simple three-lever mortice.'

25 Rugby Drive was a well-maintained semi-detached house in a row of well-maintained semi-detached houses. The garden was tidy, without any signs that the occupant was either a keen or talented gardener.

Mr Liddle walked up the path and, putting the rucksack down beside him, knelt down to take a close look at the lock.

'It's good to see it's still the original lock,' he said, speaking to the lock like an old friend.

He unfastened the straps on the rucksack and took out a cloth roll, held together by a thick elastic band which looked as old as the house and in danger of snapping at any moment. He slipped the band off the roll and put it round his left wrist. Then he unrolled the cloth on the doorstep. Inside it was an array of small tools of different sizes. Liddle selected one and inserted it into the lock. He started whistling softly to himself.

If Daykin had any doubts that Mr Liddle still had his skills, they quickly evaporated. There was a satisfying click, Liddle stopped whistling, turned the door knob and the door swung open. He looked up at them as if expecting applause.

'Would you mind waiting in the car?' asked Daykin, 'we shouldn't be long.'

'I know you and your "shouldn't be long", Tom Daykin,' said Liddle, 'that's why I brought a newspaper with me.'

He retired to the back seat of the car and, taking a pen from his pocket, started on the crossword puzzle.

Daykin and Peterson walked through the open front door and looked at what they could see of the house from the hall-way. It was like the garden, neat and in good order without any hint of chic or fashion.

'You know what you're looking for,' said Daykin, 'those three items, and anything else interesting or incriminating. Try to leave as little trace as you can that you've been here.'

They took one room each, starting upstairs and working their way from the bedrooms and bathroom down to the living-room, dining-room and kitchen. Toby Peterson found the shoes with the broken lace at the back of a shoe rack in the wardrobe of the main bedroom, but there was no sign of the other two items. They searched again, more quickly this time, as time was getting short. Still nothing. They had almost given up and were standing in the main bedroom, when Daykin saw the two-foot pole with the metal hook at the end of it leaning against the wall in the small gap between the wall and the wardrobe.

'There's a loft ladder,' he said and picked up the pole.

It was in the bathroom and they'd missed it. A small oblong trapdoor in the roof of the room with an almost invisible plastic ring at one end of it. Daykin lifted the pole vertically, put the hook into the ring and pushed sharply upwards. The trapdoor raised two inches, the locking device disengaged and he gently lowered the door down on its hinges. On what had been the upper surface of the trapdoor there was a ladder in three sections, hooking together to fit into the door's dimensions. Daykin lifted the catches and lowered each section down so that the outer one rested on the floor of the bathroom.

It was a flimsy structure and Daykin didn't want to risk his weight on it, but pride got the better of him and he gingerly put a foot on the bottom rung and began to climb.

The space below the eaves was low, cramped and had not been boarded. And it was dark, until Daykin's hand brushed against a thin cord. He pulled it and a single bare bulb hanging from the pitch of the rafters lit up. He looked around the space. There was a bit of junk, an old exercise bicycle lying on its side and a few boxes of very old cutlery and crockery. That was all he could see at first. Then he saw the white polythene bag, knotted at the top, that stood upright against the far wall.

In the confined space, and being careful to tread on the joists, Daykin made his way slowly, bending almost double and stepping sideways. 'Like a crab with a sprained ankle', as Toby Peterson described it later, he made his way across the loftspace, picking up the bag and retracing his scuttling steps. He threw the bag down on to the bathroom floor and climbed back down the ladder. Kneeling beside it, he untied the knotted polythene and, after looking into the bag, smiled at Toby Peterson. Then he pulled out a red anorak and a blue cap.

'That,' he said, 'just about sews it up.'

CHAPTER THIRTY-FOUR

T HEY put the shoes, anorak and cap into three separate evidence sacks, drove Mr Liddle back to Camleigh and returned to the station. Daykin asked the custody sergeant where Superintendent Jarvis was and was told that he was in Chief Inspector Sykes's office.

'Let's get this over with,' said Daykin to Toby Peterson and they took the evidence sacks towards the chief inspector's office.

Daykin didn't bother to knock, he walked straight in, carrying two of the sacks. Both Jarvis and Sykes looked up at him in surprise.

'Paula Josephine Sykes,' said Daykin, 'I am arresting you for the murders of Anthony Hammond and Malcolm Proctor, you do not have to say anything but it may harm your defence if you do not say something now which you later rely on in court. Anything you do say may be taken down and used in evidence. Do you understand?'

Mark Jarvis got up with a suddenness that sent his chair turning over itself in three somersaults, like a circus tumbler.

'Are you out of your mind, Daykin!'

Daykin ignored him.

'Have you anything to say?' he asked Paula Sykes evenly.

'As Superintendent Jarvis says, are you out of your mind, Inspector?' she replied defiantly. 'If this is some kind of sick joke, just get out of my office and we'll talk about it later.'

'It is not a joke, I want you to come with me to the custody unit, if you do not, I will have to handcuff you and use force. I do not want to do that.'

Chief Inspector Sykes didn't move or flinch.

'I'll give you one last chance to get out of this office and we'll put this down to a misguided sense of humour. You've got five seconds, if you're still here then I'll start disciplinary proceedings.'

'Just get out, Daykin,' said Mark Jarvis.

'I can prove that you committed two murders,' said Daykin, looking his chief inspector straight in the eye.

'On what evidence?' said Jarvis, the first seeds of doubt beginning to creep into his voice.

Daykin put the two bags he was carrying on to Paula Sykes's desk and opened the larger one. He pulled out a crumpled red anorak.

'I found this in your attic.'

Chief Inspector Sykes looked at the anorak and laughed derisively.

'So I've got an old anorak in my attic. Your point is what?'

Daykin opened the other bag, took out the blue cap and laid it on top of the anorak.

'In the same bag, I found this.'

Paula Sykes, who had seen where this was heading for some minutes, tried a different line of attack.

'You searched my house! How dare you! That settles it Daykin, I'll have you not only in front of a disciplinary committee, but drummed out of this force! You've just lost

215

your job and your pension, now get out of my sight!'

'We found these, as well,' said Daykin, taking the other bag from Toby Peterson, opening it and placing the pair of brown walking shoes on the desk.

'I believe that the broken lace on the left shoe will match the one found in the church after Tony Hammond's murder. That puts you in the church at or near the time of the murder.'

'And is that it?' said Paula Sykes, who had now seen all three bags opened. 'Is that all you've got to come charging in here and accusing me of two murders?'

'No, that's not all,' replied Daykin, 'I have a video tape of you entering Malcolm Proctor's house at about midnight on the night he died.'

If Paula Sykes had dealt with the clothing exhibits head on, this unexpected information stopped her suddenly. She stared at Daykin, her mouth slightly open and she could not think of anything to say.

Mark Jarvis had gone from outrage through shock and disbelief and back to outrage and somewhere on the journey had changed sides.

'Can you explain that, Chief Inspector?' he said.

'There must be some mistake,' said Paula Sykes.

'Commander Bennett doesn't think so,' said Daykin, knowing that that would seal the issue in Superintendent Jarvis's mind.

'I think,' Jarvis said slowly, 'you'd better go with the officers, so that we can sort this out as quickly as possible.'

Paula Sykes weighed the odds in her mind. The three men in the room were all now against her. She had two options, go quietly with them and bluff it out, or make a run for the door. Unfortunately, Daykin stood in her way. Would he hit a woman? She decided that in these circumstances, he just might. Bluff it out it was, then.

'This is a huge error and I want you to know that I will sue North Yorkshire Police and all three of you personally for all you're worth.'

They had booked Paula Sykes into the custody unit and put her in the one female cell in the small police station. Sergeant Pullan, not a man easily embarrassed, had turned red in the face when they brought her in and was crimson all through the booking in procedure.

Paula Sykes had asked for a solicitor, some high flyer from the Midlands. She wasn't one to give in easily. It would take him about two hours to reach them and so, apart from preparing an interview plan, they had time on their hands. They sat in the incident room, sorting the paperwork into two piles, those that would now be useful to them and those that wouldn't. Daykin seemed lost in his own thoughts.

'Sir,' said Toby Peterson eventually, 'if I'm going to take part in the interviews, don't you think I should know what went on?'

Daykin looked at him vacantly, then appeared to slowly come back to reality. He looked pale, tired and drained.

'Do you have a dog?' asked Daykin.

'No, sir. I haven't.'

'Would you mind coming with me while I walk mine?'

At the edge of the village a dirt track led steeply up between dry stone walls that bordered fields of barley. The path led up to Packard's Leap, a local beauty spot on the top of the hill which, it was said, gave views over ten miles in all directions. It was just one of those things local people said, no one had ever measured it.

The air was still and as they climbed the path Toby Peterson could clearly hear the old bus start up in the town below them before it set off on the local trip round five villages. To the west, dark anonymous clouds had begun to gather, it would not be long before they would bring rain, possibly a storm. Peterson hoped that Daykin didn't plan a long walk.

On the journey up the hill Daykin was silent and spent most of his time head bowed, looking down at the packed dirt of the pathway two feet in front of him. Toby Peterson thought he looked exhausted, and perhaps he was.

Eventually the path gave way to an area of grass and the steep climb became a flat open meadow overlooking a hanging valley in front of them. At the point where the land began to dip down from the meadow, someone had placed a bench. It had been there for a long time, the paint on the iron endpieces was pitted with rust and the wooden slats showed signs of woodworm. The small brass plaque that said who the bench had been erected in memory of was so dull and scratched that it could not be read, not that anyone ever tried.

Daykin sat down heavily on the bench, took off his glasses and polished the lenses with the end of his tie, all the time looking into the valley in front of him. Toby Peterson sat next to him and waited patiently. One thing he had learnt, that was that Daykin would begin in his own good time.

'I don't think that either of the churchwardens were religious men,' began Daykin, as he put his glasses back on, 'I think they needed the church as a place to meet without people getting too inquisitive.'

Toby Peterson knew that he would have to ask some questions but, for now, he was content to sit and listen while Daykin talked.

'I don't know when Michael Hilliam started dealing drugs, it was probably when his marriage broke up. The life of a

country antiques dealer can't be easy at the best of times, but
with a leech like his wife sucking at the lifeblood of the business, he can't have had much joy. He must have just been
scraping by without any foreign holidays, meals out, days at
the races, any of the little luxuries of life. Maybe the business
took a downturn and he needed money in a hurry, I don't
know, but somewhere along the line he decided that import-
ing drugs was the answer.'

'I also don't know how or when Michael Hilliam and Tony
Hammond started working together and it doesn't really
matter. I suspect that Tony Hammond still had a wide circle
of contacts in the criminal world and heard about a small-
time drug importer in his area. Possibly, he approached
Hilliam and told him he could increase his profits dramatically. Hammond knew drug wholesalers who would buy as
much as Hilliam could import and that's how the deal was set
up. Hilliam brought the drugs into the country from France,
hidden in the antique furniture in his van. Either Hammond
on his own or, more probably both of them, would then take
the drugs to Hammond's contacts who bought them. Hilliam
and Hammond then split the profits.

'The posts of churchwardens were an ideal shield. If they
were seen meeting too often at each other's houses or The
Feathers, people might start asking questions, or their conversations might be overheard. Any meetings they needed were
at the church where they said they were discussing church
business.'

'Why did Hilliam go to all the trouble of inventing
Jonathan Lister?' asked Toby Peterson.

'Two reasons. He was taking huge risks and so he wanted
to enjoy the profits by living the high life. Even though he was
going to the South of France, there was always the chance that

someone who knew him would see him and ask how he could be spending so much money. It's amazing what a change of hair colour, a pair of glasses and a different style of clothes can make. Certainly, Yvette Benastre didn't recognize his photograph. Then even if he was caught coming into the country he had a chance of persuading them that he was Lister, then disappear.'

'So why did Hammond kill him?'

'While they were equal partners and each had their own functions and contacts, the partnership worked well. But it dawned on Tony Hammond that if he knew where Hilliam was getting the drugs, he could import them and take all the profits. As soon as Hilliam agreed to take him to France, he signed his own death warrant.

'If the church had proved a safe place to meet, it must be a safe place to kill. Michael Hilliam would suspect nothing, Tony Hammond stepped behind him and stabbed Hilliam through the heart.'

'Why the cuts to the hands and feet?'

'A smoke screen. It made it look like the work of some religious fanatic. He just wanted to lay as many false trails as possible.'

'Was it just coincidence that Sykes killed the killer?'

'Very nearly, and that's what threw me. Hammond's death was made to look like another victim of the same serial killer. That was deliberate, because Paula Sykes had the perfect alibi on the night Hammond killed Hilliam, she was on duty at the police station and at least ten people could say so. She saw an opportunity to kill Tony Hammond and she took it, but to explain that I've got to start at the very beginning.'

'I had someone in Human Resources look up Paula Sykes's personnel file. I asked for a lot of files, including yours, just in case anyone was curious about me looking into a chief inspector's personnel file. She went to university where she studied chemistry, with an interest in pharmaceuticals, and that becomes important later. After she graduated, she didn't know what she wanted to do with her life, so while she made up her mind she took a short service commission in the army. That lasted three years and then she signed on for another three. Some time in the second three years she had an affair with her commanding officer, a married man nearly twenty years older than she was. She became pregnant and when the story got out she had to resign her commission. "For the good of the regiment" they said, but she noticed that the commanding officer's career went ahead as if nothing had happened. It made her very bitter.'

'After the birth of her child, a daughter, she used her university degree to get herself fast-tracked in the West Midlands Police Force. University graduates can make inspector within two years and that is what she did.'

'How is she connected to Tony Hammond?' asked Toby Peterson.

'I'm coming to that. Tony Hammond had entered the witness protection programme and had been moved from London to Birmingham. By now he was living under the name of Paul Hawkins. Early one evening, after an afternoon in the pub, he knocked over and killed a three year old child at a pedestrian crossing. The child was with her babysitter, who was also injured.'

'And the child was Paula Sykes's daughter.'

'Exactly. Hammond was arrested, but the witness protection people used their muscle to have him released, then they created a new identity for him and moved him up to North Yorkshire. A few days later, their contacts in the Home Office persuaded the Crown Prosecution Service to quietly drop any proceedings against him.'

'Paula Sykes was inconsolable, her daughter had been the centre of her life. The girl's death only added to her bitterness and she swore that Paul Hawkins would not get away it. She started making very discreet enquiries with friends in various forces. All she could find out was that a man in the witness protection programme had been moved from the Midlands to North Yorkshire at about the right time. As luck would have it, North Yorkshire were short of female chief inspectors, so she applied, they not only accepted her, but promoted her.'

When she got up here, she continued digging and found that a man called Tony Hammond had arrived in a village twenty minutes away, at the same time that Paul Hawkins disappeared from Birmingham. During his short stay at Edgbaston Police Station, as she was asked to give a witness statement about her daughter's age, she caught a brief glimpse of Hawkins. One short visit to The Feathers was enough to tell her that Hammond was the same man. From that moment she started plotting his death.'

'They say it is an ill wind that blows no man any good and the murder of Michael Hilliam was a godsend to her. I don't know how she lured Tony Hammond to the church; she might have told him that she knew about the drug dealing, because she probably did, but there was one final piece of the jigsaw to put into place. She needed a dead culprit and when she found out that Malcolm Proctor was a paedophile his death was inevitable. On the night she killed Hammond, I'm pretty certain that she telephoned Malcolm Proctor to say that she would be calling to see him. His telephone records will show if he received a call. In the meantime, because Red Malcolm was so easily recognizable by his anorak and cap, she had bought identical pieces of clothing. Now she made sure that people saw what they thought was Malcolm Proctor in the village and heading off towards the church at about the right time. She stopped at the telephone box, not only to make sure that people saw Malcolm, but she telephoned Proctor to make sure he was at home and was staying there. She could not afford to have two Malcolm Proctors walking around the village that night. Then she walked to the church where she met Tony Hammond.

'I think that, having hit him over the head, tied him up and gagged him, she made sure that his death was as slow and painful as possible. As I said, she was a very bitter woman. After leaving him in the same place and position and with the same wounds as Michael Hilliam, she made her way home, taking off the anorak and cap somewhere on the journey. She hid those in her attic until the heat had died down and she could safely get rid of them. The only mistake she made was that almost certainly in the effort of dragging the body to the nave, she broke a shoelace. That broken shoelace had me fooled again for a while. You always associate men with brown shoes, until I remembered that her hobby was walking in the Dales. Brown walking shoes.'

'And Malcolm Proctor?'

'He had to die to tie it all up into a double murder and suicide package. Very neat, case closed and no arrests. She might have got away with it, but for one thing.'

'The video camera?'

'Yes. On Friday night she went round to Proctor's just before midnight, probably apologized for missing him on the Thursday evening. He made them both a cup of coffee and she slipped some barbiturates into his cup. She knew which ones and the right amounts to use because she had studied pharmaceuticals at university. Remember that he had a poor sense of taste and wouldn't notice that something had been put into his coffee. After he was unconscious, she found some rope and cut off a length, tied it round the upstairs banister, carried Proctor halfway up the stairs, put the noose round his neck and threw him to his death. The only thing you can say is that he would not know anything about it.'

'The video camera?' prompted Peterson.

'That was one thing none of us knew about. To protect Tony Hammond, Bennett's people had set up a video camera covering his front door. It also covered across the street, so Malcolm Proctor's back door was in the line of sight. The footage isn't that good, but you can clearly see Paula Sykes going to Proctor's back door just before midnight and being let into the house.'

'Enough to convict her?'

'Who knows? That's the jury's job, not mine. I'm just glad it's all over, except for the interviews. Ready?'

'Yes, sir.'

'Then let's finish it.'

As the three of them walked down the dirt path, only the dog was disappointed to be going back to the town.